cold, thin air

A Collection of Disturbing Narratives and Twisted Tales

Volume 2

C.K. Walker

ISBN-13: 978-1517039912
ISBN-10: 1517039916

Table of Contents

MAYHEM MOUNTAIN

"In two miles take exit 19 for Valley Park Drive South." Siri chirped from my sister's phone.

"Charlotte, turn that off. I know where I'm going."

"You sure about that? I mean…it *has* been a couple decades, Mark."

"Please, like I could ever forget where Adventure Valley is. Come on, we spent every summer of-"

"There it is!" I swerved briefly into the oncoming lane as Charlotte thrust her arm in front of my face to point excitedly out the window. "There's Adventure Valley! Oh my God, what ride is that? That coaster, it was called 'Steel' something, right? No, no, wait, that's Mayhem Mountain, isn't it?"

I gently pushed my sister's arm out of my face and back over to her seat. I couldn't fault her for her excitement while I was trying so hard to control my own giddiness. It felt like we were kids again, yelling and bouncing in the back seat of my parent's car as the first shining rails and wooden planks of the park's roller coasters came into view above the treetops.

"That's the Steel Viper." I told her. "Mayhem Mountain's on the other end of the park. And that wooden coaster over there is the Excalibur."

"Oh yeah! I remember those! I was always too much of a wus to ride the viper but I rode the shit out of the Excalibur."

"Well, Charlotte, you're an adult, now. I think it's time to take on the Viper."

"As long as the contractors have tested it and given it the okay, I'm in."

That was really the question, wasn't it? We didn't know which rides had been inspected and cleared and which ones hadn't. I sent up a silent prayer that Mayhem Mountain was counted among the rides that had. I'd left Brandon several voicemails asking about it since he was the one in charge of everything. But with how fast things had been moving since we'd bought the park, I couldn't fault him for being a busy man.

If you'd told 12 year old me that my crazy, hyper, wild-eyed friend Brandon Decker would end up graduating cum laude from

Northwestern business school I would have laughed in your face. Brandon? No way. Tyler, maybe, but never Brandon. In fact, half the reason I think he choose a business designation was *because* of Adventure Valley. When the park had closed in 1989 Brandon had gathered us all together in his basement and, with a gravitas and solemnness I've never seen in him before or since, asked us to make the pact.

At the time the promise had been the most serious vow that five 12 year olds could ever make. High off of an entire summer of Adventure Valley fun, we agreed, with all the ceremony of a meeting of parliament, that we would one day come together and buy Adventure Valley Amusement Park.

Of course, back then we'd planned to just buy it and ride the roller coasters into the ground. We decided which friends from school we would let in and which enemies would be barred from the gates. It had always been *our* park, and it was only right that we should have it.

It had taken twenty years but we eventually did fulfill our promise. With a hell of a lot of pushing from Brandon (and a sizeable offer of collateral from Tyler) the bank had agreed to give us the multi-million dollar loan to buy, repair, refurbish and reopen the park. The size of the loan that the six of us were responsible for gave me nightmares for several weeks. How would this place ever turn a profit? It had been closed decades ago after operating in the red for several years. The county had experienced a high number of runaways and missing persons in the area in the last years of the 1980s. The entire region was on edge as the cases mounted and people in the area became depressed and suspicious of each other. It had absolutely killed park attendance.

But seeing the first cresting waves of roller coasters rails through the trees made me all but forget about my financial worries. This was *Adventure Valley* for Christ's sake. If we opened the gates, people would come.

"There! There, there, there – that's our exit!" Charlotte squeaked.

I pulled off the interstate and took a left under the bridge. Less than a mile later we came upon acres of the park's parking lots to our right. We turned in and drove all the way up to the front near the gates where several other cars were parked – a Lexus, a Mini Cooper, an old Chevelle and a Honda Civic – another rental car like ours.

"Looks like we're the last ones here," Charlotte said.

She was right. As we pulled up next to the Lexus I noticed a group of people standing next to the ticket booth, waving to us excitedly.

"Oh my God, is that Tyler? Jesus, he's lost some weight, he's so skinny now! And Brandon's losing his hair. Holy shit, is that Koji? Koji got hot!"

"Calm down, Paris Hilton, these guys are my friends. They're off limits to you, same rules as when we were teenagers. Besides half of them are married."

"Really...which half?"

I raised an eyebrow at Charlotte and shook my head in amused bewilderment. My little sister never had outgrown her boy craziness.

"Wait, who's that?" Charlotte asked as we got out of the car.

"What? That's Scott! You know Scott."

"Not Scott, Scott looks exactly the same. The girl *next* to Scott."

"Oh." I had put this off so long that I'd actually forgotten to tell my sister at all. "That's Dani, Scott's girlfriend."

"Dani. Dani as in Danielle...*Burcher*?"

"Well...yeah."

My sister gave me such a horrified look that you'd think I'd betrayed her to her death. But it was fleeting and quickly replaced by a sly smile.

"Fine by me. I'm sure she's not the same person she was in high school. We're all adults now, right? Now come on, let's go!"

A sigh of relief escaped my chest as I slammed the car door and followed Charlotte over to the entrance. Though I saw most of these guys every year, seeing us all here together, standing at the ticket booths of Adventure Valley, brought me a sort of happiness I hadn't experienced in many years.

"Mark-fucking-Lantice. I can't believe it." Tyler had an edgy, commanding voice that probably made his many employees shudder and scatter. But I knew him like a brother so his bravado just made me laugh.

"Can you believe it?" I asked as I gave him a hug and a slap on the back. "Back at the front gates. $15 a day doesn't seem so ridiculous now."

"Pfft, $15 a day, my ass." Brandon said as he shook my hand. "By my math, it looks like we'll be charging about $65 a day."

"I'll pay it!" Charlotte smiled as she gave Koji a hug.

"Are people really going to pay $65 a day?" Koji asked. "Even Disneyland only charges $85 and there you get access to two parks."

"How could I forget," Brandon shook his head. "One of our investors works for the mouse. Pity they won't let you design any artwork for this place."

"I'm not an artist, Bran, I'm a fucking engineer."

"Don't you mean *imagineer?*" Charlotte winked at him.

Koji sighed and shook his head. "Yeah, I guess I fuckin' do."

As Brandon and Charlotte teased Koji I made my way over to the side of the ticket booth where Scott and his girlfriend were conversing. I didn't know why Scott was being so standoffish but I thought it might have something to do with the investment. Scott, the least well off of us six, worked at his dad's collision shop and hadn't had a whole lot of money to invest. I thought maybe he was embarrassed about the money but now, watching him lean against the booth with slowly shifting eyes, I realized it wasn't that at all - Scott was just stoned. Same old Scott.

"What's up, Burnout? My brother. I haven't seen you in like 15 years."

Scott smiled and pushed off the wall to come give me a quick hug. "Hey, how's it going, man? Fuck, look at you. What's your diet, man, rabbit food and lettuce? You're not gonna get any ladies with that skinny body."

"Your mom doesn't seem to mind."

"Hey, Mark. I'm Dani. Do you remember me? Dani Burcher?" Scott's girlfriend gave me a shy smile and stuck out her hand so we could engage in a stiff handshake.

"Yeah, I think so. You were in my sister's class, right? Charlotte Lantice?"

Dani had the decency to look embarrassed. "Yeah, but we weren't really friends."

That's putting it lightly, I thought.

"We were freshmen when you guys were seniors." She added.

"Yep, I do remember that."

I decided to just get it over with. There was never a *good* time to introduce a girl to her high school bully.

I called Charlotte over and the re-introduction of the two girls, while awkward, was over pretty quickly to everyone's relief. We were all eager to get into the park. It was odd not stopping at the window for tickets and even odder to walk *around* the rusting turn-styles of the front gates. I delighted in reminding myself that we owned this place now.

Brandon gave us a tour of the park. Now so much of the geography – we all knew that inside and out – but of the hypothetical layout and reorganization of the park as he saw it.

"The Excalibur is going to need the most amount of work, according to Rich, my head contractor. A roller coaster made of wood exposed to the elements for all these years…we'll keep as much of the original structure as is safe but we might have to rebuild most of it."

"Do we have the money for that?" Scott asked loudly from where he walked behind us with Dani.

"Yeah," Tyler said. "We have the money for that."

"Ah, Mr. Moneybags. That Mini dealership treating you good?" I nudged him hard with my shoulder. Tyler stumbled but kept enough composure to push me back into a passing churro stall.

"Those *six* BMW dealerships are treating me very well."

"Well enough to serve as the sizable collateral we needed." Brandon added.

"So," Charlotte ran up behind us and threw her arms around Tyler and Koji. "Can we…ride some rides?"

"Are you kidding? Why do you think we're here?" Tyler laughed.

"I'm just here for Mayhem Mountain." I said clapping my hands and rubbing them together eagerly.

Brandon threw up his hands. "Alright, fine! I thought you guys would be interested in how your investment is coming along."

Koji snorted. "The only thing we're interested in is the projected ROI and, more importantly, which rides have passed safety inspection!"

"Oh," Brandon stopped walking and tried to look annoyed, and, failing that, he smiled. "A little over half of them are rideable."

Suddenly everybody was talking at once.

"Is Steel Viper open?"

"Yep, that one's on."

"What about Snapdragon?"

"That one is good to go, too."

"Renegade Falls?"

"The water's not turned on."

"High Roller?"

"Yes."

"Space Spin?"

"Oh yeah."

"Power Tower?"

"They're doing the inspection this week."

There was only one ride I really cared about – mine and Brandon's favorite.

"What about Mayhem Mountain?"

"Fuck. Yes." He answered to collective groans from the rest of the group.

Mayhem Mountain had always been our thing. While our friends had been happy to ride High Roller and Snapdragon into exhaustion, Brandon and I always split off toward the end of the day to ride Mayhem Mountain into the twilight hours.

"Ugh," Charlotte shuddered. "I hate that ride."

"It's boring as hell," Koji agreed. "I helped design something similar for Disneyland Hong Kong. We put it in *Fantasyland*, for fucks sake."

"Hey, that ride is awesome. It's long and it goes upside down," I argued. "Charlotte is even too scared to ride it!"

"I'm not *scared* of that ride, it just gives me the creeps. Something about it, just, I don't know, seems off."

"Alright, look. We'll start at this end of the park and work our way towards the back. That way we can ride every ride that's passed inspection - including Mayhem Mountain." Brandon said.

"And Snapdragon," Tyler added and the others nodded excitedly.

"Yes, *every* ride. And of course we can ride them, you know, as many times as we want."

"Hell yes, brother." Koji high-fived Brandon and we headed down the street toward Space Spin.

Our progress through the park was blissfully slow. Everyone wanted to ride every ride multiple times and one person always had to stay in the loading area to operate the ride.

It only took an hour or two to forget that I was a fully grown 35 year old man. Being back here, running through the line-ways with my friends, arguing who got the first row of the first car, it was like being 12 years old again.

Still, my eye was constantly drawn up over the buildings into the distance, to the back of the park where the high, gleaming rails of Mayhem Mountain shined in the unobscured sun. There would be no arguing who got front row on that coaster - it was me and Brandon. It was *always* me and Brandon.

Charlotte, Tyler and Koji were the most like children, constantly running ahead and arguing over which ride to get on next, yelling back to ask Brandon if this one or that one had been cleared by the contractors.

Brandon and I held back from the group a bit, discussing ideas and possible improvements for the park. Scott and Dani took up the rear of the group, quietly talking and lighting joints.

When we arrived at the Enterprise, a simple ride that consisted on spinning cars on a circular track, I offered to flip the switch while the rest of the group rode to excess. The Enterprise always made me sick when we were kids. Brandon offered to stay on the platform with me to chat while everyone else boarded the cars.

I flipped the switch to start the ride and as the cars spun away from the loading area, the Enterprise's signage came into view. I sighed. All day I had been trying to ignore the bright graffiti sprayed all over the park but the words painted over the signage for the Enterprise were impossible to ignore.

Where did the missing kids go?

And the rest of the graffiti in the park was much the same. Most said things like: "Where are they?", "Runaway Row", "Find Ryan Kinskey", and "The Missing are now Dead". Similar sayings could be found in town sprayed across a few dilapidated buildings in the industrial district.

Brandon's eyes avoided the sign but I could tell he was thinking about it, too.

"Do you think the reason they shut this park down, I mean, do you see that being an issue for park attendance?" I asked as casually as I could.

Brandon was quiet for a few moments as he waited for the ride to slow to a stop so he could flip the switch again.

"Nah, I don't think so. Low attendance issues aren't actually what shut the park down."

"They aren't?" This surprised me.

"Nope. When we were negotiating the sale of the park, I was given access to the park's financials in the 80s."

"So they weren't operating at a loss?"

"Oh they were. But this park has operated in the red since opening day in the 70s. Half of their revenue was being fed back into something called 'county services', whatever that is. The bank couldn't tell me and believe me, I tried to find out."

"County services…" I mused.

"Yep. Bizarre. And according to the paperwork the park was closed because the owner didn't want to live here anymore. And he couldn't be bothered to wait for a decent offer on the property so he just let the bank foreclose on it."

"So he was a rich guy." I leaned back against the railing to stretch my back. "And an idiot."

"Yes – to an extreme in both cases. The owner of the park was Abel Bisette."

"Bisette? Related to that French billionaire, I'm guessing?"

Brandon nodded. "Michael Bisette. He built this park for his son in the 1971. Abel was never really what we would call 'business inclined'. In fact I've always heard him described as 'simple'."

"I can't believe the son of a billionaire lives in this area."

"Well, not anymore. He moved on decades ago."

I shook my head in disbelief. Who would ever have thought that our simple little park was owned by a famous billionaire's son? Hell, I may have even sat next to him on rides and had no idea!

"You guys want to go again?" Brandon yelled to the others as the ride again came to a stop.

"I'm ready to move on," Koji yelled back. "Anybody want to ride again?"

"Nope!" a chorus of voices replied.

It was near 5 o'clock when we finally arrived at Mayhem Mountain. As the sun began to set a familiar panic and urgency welled in the pit of my stomach. It took a moment for me to realize that we didn't have to leave when the park closed this time – because the park didn't close. We could stay here riding rise until the sun rose tomorrow if we wanted to!

cold, thin air vol. 2

As I eagerly approached the turn-style for Mayhem Mountain Tyler spoke up behind me. "Listen, can we run into town and grab something to eat before we ride Mayhem?"

"You really want to ride Mayhem *after* we eat?" Asked Koji. "Good point."

"It only goes upside down once," Dani rolled her eyes.

"Twice," I said. "Don't forget the inline roll."

"Yep, twice." Scott said. "Plus it's a two minute ride. If your food isn't sitting well, you've got a long wait 'til it's over."

"Look," I said, "Let's ride it a couple times and then go eat. When we come back we'll see how we feel."

Everyone nodded and we started walking through the line-ways up to the platform. When we reached the loading dock, I was excited to see our favorite green car sitting on the track.

"Front!" Brandon and I yelled simultaneously as soon as the train cars came into view. Everyone behind us groaned.

"I'm staying here," Charlotte said. "I'll just work the launch pad thingy."

"Still scared after all these years, Char?" Scott teased her.

"Shut up, Burnout."

Scott laughed and tousled her hair before running and jumping into the first car behind Brandon and I. Dani got in next to him and then Tyler and Koji took the second car. We pulled the shoulder restraints down and they locked in place.

"Ready?" Charlotte asked.

"Yep!" Brandon yelled back, "Send the car through!"

Charlotte pulled the lever and the brakes disengaged. As the car moved forward I turned to Brandon.

"Did we get the green car on purpose?" I yelled to him as the coaster clacked around the load platform and began the clattery climb up the first lift hill.

"Yep! We sent cars through here all morning but I made sure Rich knew to leave the Green Machine in the loading bay."

"Awesome."

As the train climbed up the lift hill I made no attempt to hide my utter glee. I looked out over the expansive park and couldn't believe it was mine. Every track, every car, every turn-style, every *screw*, from the front gate to the overflow parking lot in the back, it was all ours. How I wished I could go back in time and tell a young me waiting in the two hour line for Mayhem Mountain – one day, you will OWN this place. And as we crested the hill and the train fell into the first drop, I realized I essentially *had* gone back in time. At least, I was screaming like a 12 year old, as was everyone else behind me.

We dipped into the first tester hill and then banked hard and up, to the second lift hill. We dropped from there, down into the vertical loop, banked around a set of gift ships, up briefly and then down a small hill into the inline roll. When we arrived back at the loading bay we were all screaming and whooping. Charlotte didn't even have to ask, just smiled at us and sent us through again.

We went twice more before we finally got off the ride. Koji walked over to check out the control panel while the rest of us taunted my sister.

"You sure you don't want to go, Char? It's awesome."

"Nah, I'm good. I have no problem being the carny for this ride." She laughed.

"Come on, Charlotte, just one time. One time and we'll leave you alone." Tyler urged.

"No, no, no, no, no. No way. Not interested. I'll ride anything else, though!"

"Hey, do you guys know what Track B is?" Koji asked.

"Track B? What do you mean?" Brandon walked over to Koji at the control board and raised an eyebrow. "That's weird."

"It's probably just the track they use to get the cars into the storage bay," Scott said with a shrug.

"No," Koji said. "That's called a transfer track. Track B has to be something else."

"Yeah, well I've been on this ride enough times to know that there is no other track."

"Yep," Tyler agreed with me. "He has."

"So…should we try it?" Brandon tested.

"Fuck no." Said Charlotte. "If you don't know what Track B is that means the contractors don't know about it either. Which means it hasn't been inspected in at least 20 years. That's suicide."

"Look," Koji said, "if there is indeed a Track B than even the most incompetent of engineers would have found it during an inspection."

"And Rich cleared this entire ride," Brandon nodded. "It's probably just the ride in reverse. We're good."

"Well, we're in," announced Scott from the other side of the track, though Dani didn't look quite like she agreed with him.

"Mark?" Tyler asked.

"Yeah, I guess I'm in. What the worst that could happen: we get funneled into a repair bay?"

"Alright, then I'm in too." Tyler said hesitantly.

Koji shrugged. "Here goes nothing."

He flipped the switch over to Track B and a moment later a loud metallic scraping some distance away filled the park. The sound lasted almost a minute. I studied the familiar silver roller coaster under the pink sky of the setting sun but I saw no physical changes to the track. I looked over at Brandon and a shrug of his shoulders told me he didn't either.

"Shall we?" Scott asked gesturing to the train cars we'd just disembarked. I gave Charlotte a questioning look but she shook her head emphatically no. So it was just the six of us again.

"It's only right you two take the bow of the ship." Tyler gave a mock salute. "O Captains, my captains."

I laughed and hopped into the right side of the front row. Brandon crawled into the seat next to me. Tyler and Koji got in behind us and Scott and Dani took the back. We pulled the shoulder bars down and they locked into place.

"Are you sure about this?" Charlotte asked when everyone was settled.

Dani said something from her place a few rows back but all I heard was Brandon yelling "Pull it!"

The brakes released and the train rolled away from the platform and into the twilight of dusk. The lights had lit up on the track while we'd been arguing and the roller coaster looked absolutely beautiful. I was filled with awe and reverence at what this place truly meant to my friends and me. It was a symbol of our youth and innocence and blissful ignorance of the world. It was our own little bubble of happiness.

The coaster again climbed the lift hill and from the top Brandon and I studied the track but in those few seconds I saw no difference. Brandon looked over and I shook my head at him disappointedly. By the time we reached the vertical loop halfway through the ride it was clear that there was no Track B. But it was hard to be upset because I was still on Mayhem Mountain and still found it an impossible challenge not to smile.

We banked around the now brightly lit gift shops, up the small tester hill and then back down to the inline roll. Except…the inline roll was suddenly above us. We'd missed it. Instead the track now descended into a large, square hole in the ground behind the gift shops – and we were headed directly into it.

I was in too much shock to scream or even move. The black hole swallowed us in an instant and we descended into complete darkness. I felt a comfortable pressure leave my shoulders and realized that the shoulder bars had released. I gripped the front lip of the ledge of my seat and heard the terrified screams of my friends behind me as the coaster suddenly spun into what felt like an inline roll. I was too scared to do anything but hold on for dear life though some part of my brain registered that the g-forces of the roll probably would have been enough to keep me in my seat if I had let go. Probably.

We came out of the inline roll and dropped again - hard. As the roller coaster dropped the room suddenly lit up around us and I saw the track below arcing up into a light tester hill. As we hit the bottom of the hill the shoulder bars lowered mechanically. The car went over the small tester hill and then braked to start up another tall lift hill. I took my first breath since dropping through the ground and looked around, tuning out the screams of Dani and Tyler behind me.

We were in what can be described as a cavernous room and I only assume it stretched to the farthest reaches of the park above. There were lots of vertical loops, high drops and sharp curves that put the track perpendicular to the ground. Throughout the entire sublevel building lamps dotted the wall every 30 feet. They put out a dreary, yellowed glow for as far as the eye could see. But many were burnt out and in parts the track disappeared into darkness.

But in the dull, yellow edges of the light I saw something in the distance that registered in me a horror beyond death. Far away from us, within a section of shadowy track, I saw the high crest of a peak hill which almost reached the ceiling of the giant room. And then the track just…ended.

Suddenly the horrible reality of the world outside my mind began to bleed in. Dani was screaming uncontrollably, Tyler was crying, bawling even, Koji was yelling at Brandon who was looking straight at me, hitting my leg hard and repeating my name. As the cars continued to climb I finally gave him my attention. I didn't want to be alone in the fear anymore.

"What is this?" was all I could think of to say.

"We have to get off this ride. We have to get off this ride, Mark."

"I fucking know, man."

"We're going to die."

"I fucking know, man!" I yelled as we reached the top of the lift hill and dropped over the other side. I squeezed my eyes shut until I felt the shoulder bars once again release and I bit my lip to keep from crying. I opened my eyes and choked as I watched the track ahead up us bend up into a vertical loop. I reached up and tried to pull the shoulder bar down but it was locked in place.

"Hang on! Hang on to the seats!" I yelled as loud as I could.

As we approached the loop I felt the brakes engaging, slowing the car, and a tow cable catch beneath my feet. We were being pulled up through the loop, but too slowly for gravity to keep us in our seats.

As the train began to invert I felt my feet rise from the floor of the car. My hair fell over my face and my butt left the seat. I closed my eyes and tried to block out the screams of terror from behind me. I concentrated on my death grip of the ledge of my seat as we rounded the track. We remained upside down for what felt like eternity. Finally the pressure began to ease, my butt dropped to my seat and my feet to the floor. The white noise subsided from my ears and I heard Koji's screaming.

"Tyler! Fuck, fuck, he fell out. Fuck, he fell, he's dead, man, he's dead."

"He hit the track down there." Brandon yelled at me, wide-eyed and crazy looking. I was finally seeing the Brandon from my youth. The shoulder bars descended again, this time locking in tighter.

We came out of loop and sped up and down several tester hills. I tried to study the track ahead of us as we went through the safer parts. I thought I saw water reflecting off of metal somewhere in the distance. Brandon sobbed in his seat.

"Mark, what are we gonna do? I don't wanna die, man. I don't wanna fucking die."

"I don't know. I don't know what to do. I'm sorry, I'm fucking scared, too." I answered him.

We banked around a corner of the room and the shoulder bars released again. This time we dove into a curve that put the left side of the train parallel to the ground – and it was a long drop to the ground. I gripped the edge of the seat tightly as before but this time I kept my eyes open and was able to catch Brandon as he began to slip out of his seat.

By the time the train righted itself, I couldn't tell who'd been lost. Most of the screaming behind me had turned to loud sobbing or silence. The shoulder bar didn't reengage and I felt the car's brakes slow the train down again. I didn't have to even look up to know what was coming next.

It was another vertical loop. This one was larger and taller and I knew we'd be upside down for longer. Someone behind me began screaming again, Dani I think, as I tried to take measured breaths and position my aching hands back under the lip of the seat. Brandon did the same and looked over at me as the car started up the loop with tears streaming down his face.

"I don't wanna die in here, man."

I shook my head back at him because I couldn't think of anything to say.

I felt myself start to cry as we reached the tipping point of the loop and my feet again left the floor. Before we were even completely upside down I felt my back begin to slip down the seat. I thought if I lost my grip, I could try to grab for the shoulder bars as I fell.

The car suddenly stopped and I opened my eyes to see we were completely inverted. I grunted loudly at the pain and immense effort it was taking to keep my grip on the seat. The car started to move again slowly and I heard Brandon say something to me. I looked over at him just before he slid out of the car. One second he was there, next to me, and the next he was falling, falling away to the end of his life.

I saw Brandon try to grab the shoulder bar on the way out but it slipped right out of his hands. I watched him fall and I saw him break his back on the track below and he stopped moving. I stared down at him as the car continued to move slowly around the loop and he stared back up at me, dead, or dying. By the time the car hit him on the way out of the loop, he was completely gone.

The shoulder bars re-engaged and we went through a dreadfully long period where nothing happened. We were secured in our seats by the restraints as the coaster spent what felt like several minutes racing over hills, banks, curves, even an inline roll.

With less adrenaline pumping through my veins, I felt the shock begin to wear off. It was replaced by a panic and fear unlike I'd ever experienced. I decided that was the point of this section of track: to build and facilitate an unbearable fear.

I felt the brakes engage finally and I looked ahead to find the loop we were surely entering but there was none. We were high, almost to the top of the ceiling and we slowed to a stop on a straightaway. Directly ahead was a drop and at the bottom of the hill, a series of four different tracks, with a transfer stack just before they split off. Each track had five or so feet of color – red, orange, green and blue – before racing off in different directions.

I felt an urgent shaking of my shoulder and turned around to hear what Koji was saying.

"Which track are we connected to?"

I looked at the transfer stack.

"Green."

"Where does green go?" It was hard to hear him over the sound of Dani's sobbing from the second car. I tried to trace the green track through the building, constantly losing it and finding it again. I wasn't sure, but it seemed to end at the lift hill I'd seen earlier. The hill with no track at the top.

"It ends at that hill," I yelled back at him and pointed. Dani cried louder.

"Fuck."

While we were stopped I rubbed my hurting hands together. As I looked down at them I noticed something new in the car. At some point a small, blinking panel had flipped over in the wall at the front of the car. It had four colored buttons and an old analog timer. The timer was so old and damaged that though the numbers were clearly changing I couldn't see what they were.

"We get to choose," I said and explained what I was looking at.

"Can you see which track ends where?" Koji asked.

I followed all the track as best I could but the rails circled and slid in between each other. It was hard to tell which track went where.

"I think the blue track ends in that big pool in the corner. The red track ends in a wall coming out of a drop and the orange one just drops into a hole in the floor like the one we came down here through. I think."

"There's no way out, dude," said Scott from the second car. His voice was unsettlingly calm. "They're just telling us how we're going to die."

"We can still find a way out of this." I answered quietly, more to myself than to him.

"Choose the pool," Scott said, and I could hear the tears in his voice. "I've heard drowning isn't an awful death." Dani sobbed louder.

"No! Choose the hole in the floor," said Koji. "It's possible it drops down into another cavern like this. There might be more track which means more time to figure out how to live."

"You don't think we'd be the first to choose that option, do you?" Scott asked him. "And no one that went missing ever came back. There's just more death in that hole."

"I don't want to die like this," Koji begged. "And at least it's a chance."

Dani cried in the back and offered no suggestion. It seemed the decision was up to me and I had to make it fast.

I knew I didn't want to die by dropping off the track. I didn't want to drown. Perhaps the quickest death was the wall. More than likely we would all be killed instantly. Less suffering, less time to think about our fates. But the truth was, I wasn't even entirely sure that I had followed the tracks right anyway. It was all educated guesswork and my time was up.

"The orange. Let's go down to the second floor, if there is one."

Scott and Dani said nothing and Koji choked out the last words I'd ever hear him say.

"Push it before it chooses for us."

Before I could think about it any longer I pushed the orange button and committed us to whatever death it led to. We heard the metallic scraping of the track transferring below. Once the orange track was securely connected, the brakes on the car released and the train rolled slowly toward the drop. Dani started screaming again.

As we dropped down the hill I got a better view of the orange track. There was a vertical loop ahead that didn't look as high as the others we'd been through. If fact, it looked like there was a chance a fall from it wouldn't necessarily kill us. *If* it wasn't an optical illusion and *if* the shoulder bars disengaged for that loop we might have a shot at living through this. I yelled back to everyone behind me.

"Let yourself fall out of the loop, the one up there!"

No one responded to me, which didn't matter because I didn't think I'd have the courage to let go of the seat anyway.

We raced along the track in and out of banks and curves. When we passed along the pool and I forced myself to look down into it. Below the water's surface the track ended above an even deeper pool. I could see the shadows of several coaster cars at the very bottom.

I suddenly felt the brakes engage and I realized we were coming to the loop. I tested the shoulder bar by pushing up on it but it stayed locked. I was somewhat relieved in that moment to know I wouldn't have to make the decision to fall out now or gamble on the orange track. The feeling was short lived as a moment later the restraints began to release.

As we started up the loop I gripped the lip of the seat tightly and turned my head back to look down. The ground looked much farther away that I'd thought it would. We were very high and I only hoped the ground was made of the loosely packed dirt it looked like. The seconds slipped by, I was running out of time. I had to choose now — the fall or the hole.

I choose the fall.

I squeezed the plastic lip of the seat one more time before I gave myself over to gravity. As I felt myself begin to slide up the seat I yelled at the others to let go and fall out of the car. Then I squeezed my eyes shut and felt my head crack the shoulder bar on the way out.

It wasn't a long, agonizing, slow motion fall like I thought it'd be. It was over in an instant: one moment I felt an intense pain as my head hit the shoulder bar and in that same breath I was on the ground, solid dirt underneath me. I hadn't even had the time to consider the possibility that I'd hit the track below on the way down but now I was staring up at it and as my vision blurred and cleared I watched the green cars speed over the track above me.

The pain didn't hit me all at once. I had one long, blissful second before I felt it. And then I was in agony.

I'd hoped my body was so in shock that I wouldn't feel much of the pain but I felt it all. I concentrated on keeping my eyes open and trying to catalog the damage. There was blood on my clothes but I didn't know what part of my body it was coming from. I heard screaming as well but I didn't know if it was in my head or coming from my friends as they approached the end.

I didn't want to move, didn't think it was safe to move, but I knew I had to, if only to pull out my phone. With trembling fingers I pulled the thing from my pocket and brought it to my face, trying to focus on the screen. But it was shattered and refused to even turn on. I threw it away from me and then I realized the silence.

Their ride had ended.

With a great amount of effort I rolled over onto my stomach and dragged my broken body across the ground toward where I thought I remembered seeing the hole. I crawled for what seemed like hours and maybe it was. Sometimes I tried to stand or even kneel but the pain in my back and ribs was too great. I was dizzy and almost passed out several times from shock and pain but eventually I made it to where the track disappeared into the ground. I pulled myself to the edge of the hole and looked down inside.

The track ended just below the surface.

It was a natural shaft with walls made of rock. I didn't know how deep it went and I didn't want to. It was a fate I'd only narrowly escaped. But then I thought about the fact that my friends were down there and maybe someone survived.

"Koji?" My voice echoed loudly down the shaft. No answer.

"Scott?" Nothing.

I reached for a small scrap of metal nearby and dropped it down the hole. I estimate it took half a minute to land and when it did it was with a *clang* as it hit something else made of metal. The deadly sound echoed up the shaft and out into the cavernous room and I realized this place was built with acoustics in mind. I rolled over onto my back and studied everything I could see from where I was, fighting to deny my body's desire to pass out again. I felt nothing but numbness when I finally saw it - a long, panoramic window in the far wall. The moment I realized what Track B was for and I let myself slip away into the darkness.

I remember very little of my rescue. There were tons of people in uniform and my sister yelling and pain - lots of pain. I was in and out on the way to the hospital but I remember passing through the room behind the window at some point. And from my stretcher, through the chaos, I saw in that room a single chair facing the window. It was covered in a deep layer of dust.

I was never visited by anyone official, let alone asked to give a statement. Charlotte stayed by my side at the hospital for months while I recovered. She wouldn't say much about that day although she finally did tell me something.

Charlotte said that the EMTs wouldn't let her ride with me to the hospital and the cops wouldn't give her a lift either. She was confused at their briskness and lack of sympathy but then someone offered her a ride – a stranger. On the drive she'd been spoken to by two people who had somehow convinced her to forget about what had happened and to convince me of the same. However they had threatened her was so effective that she begged me to agree. And I did – at the time.

I am still recovering from my injuries and just now learning to walk without aid. And I never saw Mayhem Mountain again. The loan defaulted and Adventure Valley was bought up by an unknown LLC which bulldozed it and built a block of apartments over the top. They're sit empty to this day.

I don't like the dark anymore. It reminds me of the horror my friends experienced as they looked at the track ahead of them and saw it end before they disappeared into that hole. I try not to think of what they must have felt as they fell down the shaft in complete darkness, strapped in their seats, waiting for the terrible, inevitable end. I wish I'd chosen the pool, if only to save them from that fate.

As for the billionaire's son, Abel Bisette was only 'simple' in the fact that he was a man of simple tastes. And he still is.

I looked him up once, only a few years ago. He owns several amusement parks now, all small but sizable enough to be popular in their specific regions. In fact, one is not very far from where I live now. I see it sometimes as I drive by on the way to work.

I've thought about going many times, just to check, just to see. But then I realized that I probably didn't need to search all the rides in the park to know.

Because it is a certainty that underneath the midway, below the carnival games and overpriced food stands, Track B lies in the dark listening to the laughter and delighted screams of the patrons above. It waits patiently. It waits silently. Perhaps it waits for you.

BLUE RIDGE:
A SEQUEL TO PARADISE PINE

"Do you know where we're supposed to park? Ingrid. Hey, did Mel tell you where to park?"

"What?" I turned away from the window and flashed Lloyd an apologetic smile. "Sorry, I was just watching something...out...the..."

"Ingrid."

"Sorry! God, it's been a long week. No, she didn't say but since we're the last ones there, I would assume we just park next to everyone else."

"Actually, we're not," Moss piped up from the back seat. "Ben just texted that he's still on the 87."

"Guy sells two songs to Maroon 5 and now he thinks he can make us wait around like he's a damn celebrity," Lloyd mumbled.

"Please, Ben's never been on time to anything in his life. Isn't that half the reason the band broke up?" Moss laughed.

"Nah, the band broke up because Ash got deployed and Ben was too good for it anyway."

Moss smiled and sat back in his seat.

Lloyd and I had been together for four years and he'd been unemployed for three of them. He'd put everything he had into his band and for a while it looked like Vintage Truth was going to make it. Then one day his guitarist, Ashley, up and joined the Marines and his drummer/songwriter, Ben, sold one of the band's songs to a recording label for an ungodly amount of money. Lloyd said he'd forgiven them but nevertheless had spent the subsequent years wandering aimlessly through his life.

It was an obvious sore spot for him and no one mentioned Vintage Truth around Lloyd anymore. Well, no one but Moss.

"So where did Melanie find this place?" Moss nudged the back of my seat with his foot.

"Actually, Ashley found this one. He said he wanted something on Blue Ridge Mountain."

"I'm surprised he had the time to book it, he's only been back from Iraq for a couple weeks."

"It only takes a few minutes on the internet."

"Maybe for you, Ing. But the last cabin you rented us had rats the size of Lloyd's mom's dildos."

"-those weren't rats!"

"-fuck you, Moss."

Moss laughed. "Just sayin'!"

"Those were mice. And I'm sure he found it on the same website where I find all of my cabins." I rolled my eyes at Moss.

"Yeah," Lloyd complained. "But this place is like 13 miles from town and the last 3 miles have been unpaved. You sure he's not bringing us back here to kill us all?"

"I'm not entirely certain, Lloyd, but if he is there's not much we can do about it at this point." I said sarcastically.

"Oh come on, babe, you know love me." Lloyd winked at me. I smiled at him and leaned over to give him a kiss. Just as my lips brushed his cheek, Moss sat up and thrust his arm in between us to point into the distance.

"There it is! Finally."

The cabin was much bigger and older than it looked in the pictures Melanie had shown me. The home was three stories tall and built eloquently into the side of the mountain. It had a small clearing serving as a "front yard" and a dark, dense tree line beyond it.

"Wow, we're really in the middle of nowhere..." I said to myself as Lloyd pulled into the small, dirt parking lot.

"Yep. That means we can be as drunk and loud as we want and there are no neighbors to complain."

"Yeah," I nodded, "I guess. I just hope we don't get the bottom floor bedroom."

"I'll take the bottom bedroom," Moss said from the backseat. "I need a quiet place to sext Lloyd's mom."

"Moss, I fucking-"

Lloyd threw the car in park and lunged into the backseat just as Moss pushed open the door and ran for the staircase up to the main floor of the cabin. I shook my head as I watched Lloyd twist around, open his door and sprint out of the vehicle, laughing. Moss was inside the front door by the time Lloyd reached the bottom stair.

I got out and popped the trunk, tugging on the heavy, beer-laden cooler inside. After being cooped up with those two for three hours, I needed a drink.

I was struggling pretty hilariously when I heard an amused voice behind me.

"I can't decide if I'd rather have the beer or the view."

I spun around and pushed my ball cap up out of my eyes.

"Fucking Ash, get over here and help me."

He laughed, striding casually over to the back of the car and I threw my arms around him in a tight hug. It had been 14 long months since I'd last seen my childhood friend.

"Hey, Ing, how've you been?"

"Good," I said letting him go. "Have you seen your mom and dad since you've been back?"

Our families had always been close and I knew from talking to my mom how excited his parents were to see him.

"No, they're flying out here next weekend. I'm picking them up from the airport like a good son."

"Good." I gave him a radiant smile. "So we have you all to ourselves for the next five days then."

"Well, you'll have to fight Mel on that. If it were up to her I'd never leave the bedroom."

"Oh, god, gross, Ash. I don't need to hear about that shit, you're like my brother."

Ash laughed. "Hear about *what?* I didn't say anything."

"Don't even imply it. Whatever you and your girlfriend do-"

"Holy shit, as I live and breathe, is that the distinguished Ashley Allender?! What are you doing down there?" Lloyd peered down at us from the second floor deck.

"That's Lance Corporal Allender to you. And I'm helping your girlfriend unload the car since you're an asshole."

"Oh fuck, I forgot, hang on!"

Lloyd set his beer on the railing and ran inside as Moss leaned against the door jamb shaking his head at Lloyd as he passed by.

"He really is an asshole," I laughed.

*

It was an hour and a few beers later when Ben finally pulled up in his brand new H2. Ash and Moss took turns hurling insults at Ben's new "Pavement Princess" as Melanie and I sat back on the deck and tried not to laugh.

As soon as Ben walked out onto the deck, Lloyd thrust a beer into his hand.

"Finally! Now that we're all here I call for a toast to our asshole friend Ash."

"Oh yes! A toast to assholes!" Mel sprang up beside me and pulled Ash back into the circle as shook his head ardently and backed away from us.

"Come on, guys, this is embarrassing. Don't fucking toast me."

"That's the whole reason we're here, baby!"

"Mel..."

"Come on, Ash," I teased. "Let your friends toast you. We haven't seen you in forever."

"Fuck, alright, make it quick." Ash tried to look annoyed but failed hilariously.

"I'll start, then." Ben held up a bottle of his fancy Trappist beer and everyone else followed suit.

"Well, you are the lyricist." Mel rolled her eyes playfully and pulled Ash's arm around her.

"Ashley, what else can I say but thank you for both your service and the great honor of being your friend. We're glad you're home."

We clinked our bottles together as Moss murmured: "That was disappointing."

It was many cheers and many rounds later when I found myself alone with a drunken Moss and Ash.

"I- I'm so proud of you, Ash." I stuttered, putting a friendly arm around him. "I wasn't sure about all of this when you told me you'd enlisted but dammit if I'm not honored as hell to call you my friend."

"Thank you, but honestly all the praise sorta makes me uncomfortable."

"Really? Why?"

"Because I don't know....most of the last 14 months was just training. I was only in Iraq for about 6 of it, in actual combat, for less."

"Yeah, you must have seen some shit, though." I nodded my head at him.

Ash was quiet for a beat too long and even in my drunken state I could tell the air had shifted. Moss - who was excellent at reading people and situations - broke the tension before it got too thick.

"I've seen some shit too, man."

Ash and I looked up at him as he took a long, intense swig of his beer.

"Lloyd's mom just sent me nudes."

Ash and I laughed and looked over at Lloyd, who was staring down at his phone, shaking his head.

"One fucking day, Moss." He said without looking up.

"Oh, come on, man. That's what I do. I'm a stand up comedian; it's my job to make people laugh."

"A failing stand up comedian who wears makeup even when he's *off* stage." I added with a wink at Moss.

"No, I most certainly do-"

"Ben, you alright, man?" Ash interrupted and we all looked over to the corner of the deck where Ben was standing, looking out into wood.

"Ben."

He didn't look at us, but motioned Ash over with his hand. They stood in the corner and exchanged quiet words.

"What is it?" Mel asked after a minute.

"I think it was just a bear." Ash answered her.

"*Just* a bear? A fucking bear?" Mel pulled her hoodie tighter around her.

"Well, we are in the middle of the woods, darling." Moss said casually from his chair.

"Yep, bears are to be expected out here," Ash said, and gave Ben a look I couldn't translate.

"Fuck that, I'm going inside. A bear could climb up on the deck you know," Mel strode quickly over to the sliding door.

"That's why you never come out into the forest without a gun." Ash said from the corner of the deck, and he continued to stare out into the trees.

*

The next day no one got up until 11AM. By the time I walked out into the living room Moss, Ash and Ben were up guzzling down water and wearing sunglasses to block out the bright sun that was streaming through the large, floor to ceiling windows. Melanie was cheerfully making pancakes in the kitchen and Lloyd was out on the deck smoking a cigarette. "Last to the party, Ingrid. Means you have to go upstairs to my suitcase and grab more Excedrin."

"Fuck you, Ashley." I murmured as I dropped onto the sofa and threw my arm over my eyes.

"Guys!" Mel sang out from the kitchen. "We should go on a hike today!"

Her suggestion was met with a collection of unappreciative groans.

The hike didn't happen until around 2 o'clock, after I'd had a shower and the boys had had a hair of the dog.

It was beautiful out, cool for that time of year, but no snow yet. The hiking trail was well marked and easy to follow and I was glad for the fresh air. We were loud and boisterous but no one was around to hear us anyway. Our chance of seeing any animals out in nature, though, was laid completely nil. They could likely hear us coming from miles away.

I was at the back of the group with Ben and Lloyd. Ash had naturally taken the lead followed by Mel and Moss.

"How's the music industry, Ben?" I heard Lloyd ask, nonchalantly.

"It's good, man." Ben seemed to hesitate for a minute. "But it needs more actual *talent.*"

"Yeah, I've heard what's on the radio, I can't disagree with that." Lloyd laughed.

"I mean it needs YOU, man."

"Me? I'm quit making music, you know that. I'm concentrating on writing my book."

Book? I'd never heard Lloyd talk about a book.

"Your book?"

"Yeah. I'm writing a book. In the high fantasy genre."

"Oh. You know you didn't have to, though. Quit music."

"Are we really gonna have this argument again, man? The band broke up, Ben, what do you want me to do. That was years ago."

"It didn't break up, Lloyd; you gave up on Vintage Truth. Yes, Ash left but you still had me, we could have found another bass player." Ben said, accusingly.

My ears perked up. This was a version of the story I hadn't heard before.

"You'd just sold 'Tempered Hearts' to Reprise. You think I was going to hold you back?"

"You weren't holding me back, Lloyd. All I wanted was to keep Vintage Truth going - you knew that and you left anyway. I told you I wanted to invest that money back-"

"Ben!" Ash's voice called out ahead of us. "Can you come up here?"

"One second," Ben said, and then disappeared to the front of our group. I raised an eyebrow at Lloyd.

He shook his head and looked away from me, pulling his pack of cigarettes from his pocket.

"You know," I laughed, "the fresh mountain air-"

"Fuck the fresh mountain air." Lloyd muttered.

The smile dropped from my face. We stood in an uncomfortable silence listening to Moss tell Melanie about a terrible date he'd had until Ben returned.

"What did Ash want with you?" I asked.

"He...nothing."

"Oh, come the fuck on, Ben, what did he want?" Lloyd asked.

"He said someone was following us."

I stopped and turned around. "What? Really? I haven't seen anyone."

"That's what he said and he wanted me to watch the back of the group."

"And did you see him? The guy following us?"

"I didn't see shit, Ingrid."

"That's fucking weird."

"Honestly, I'm not entirely sure Ash saw anything at all."

Lloyd stared out into the woods around us and ran a hand through his mess of hair. "Do you think he's still adjusting to being back?"

"Yeah, I do," Ben admitted. "He was in an active war zone for four months. I think he might need more than a couple weeks to get used to being home."

*

Over the next two days a thick blanket of tension descended over the cabin. Ash spent most of his time walking around the house, staring out the windows and going on solo hikes. Lloyd stayed in our room every day until the sun went down writing his book and Mel ferried back and forth between the two trying to get them to loosen up and socialize.

As for Moss, Ben and I, we spent our days getting drunk and trying to break up the tension. When that failed, I started looking around the cabin for books to read since clearly it was going to be a long week.

After a thorough search, I'd learned the only literature in the house was a Pictionary Dictionary and what looked like a handwritten diary.

"What the hell do you think this is?" I asked nobody in particular.

"It's like a journal where past cabin guests write about their experiences." Ben said from the couch nearby.

"Huh. Well, I do need something to read."

"I wouldn't bother," Ben shook his head. "There's never anything interesting in those things."

I shrugged and threw the book on the kitchen counter, then went to grab another beer.

On the fourth day of our trip, I decided to get up early and make breakfast. I was upset that everyone seemed so down when this was supposed to be a fun trip to welcome Ashley home. It was time to make eggs and mimosas and change the waning tide.

When I walked into the kitchen at daybreak, I was surprised to see Ash standing over the sink staring out the window intently.

"Morning, Ash. What in the hell are you doing up so early?"

He didn't answer me. I went to stand beside him and tried to follow his gaze.

"What are we looking at?"

"There's three of them." He said without moving.

"Three of what?"

"I don't know."

"Okay..." I backed away from the window. "Are you okay, man?"

Ash suddenly pointed out into the forest. "There! There's one right there! Did you see it?"

I peered cautiously over his shoulder. I searched the wood but didn't see anything out of the ordinary.

"What am I looking for? The bear?"

"There was no bear."

"What was it, then?"

Ash didn't say anything for a moment. "It's hard to describe."

"Alright. Can you draw me a picture?" I laughed. Ash finally looked away from the window.

"Yeah, I can."

He grabbed the cabin journal off the counter where I'd thrown it the day before and tore out a blank page. Grabbing the nearest pen, Ash made a handful of strokes and handed the paper to me.

I looked at in confusion. "This is a stick figure."

Ash nodded and went back to looking out the window. "Sometimes they seem to disappear, but they always reappear a few seconds later, close than where they were before."

"Okay... Ashley, this, ah, stick man thing, it has a perfectly round head like this?" I pointed to his drawing. Ash nodded.

"And little stick arms and legs? And a little stick body?"

Ash suddenly spun toward me and grabbed my shoulders. "Ingrid, I don't want Melanie sleeping in the room upstairs anymore. I can hear them at night. They walk around on the roof and tap on the sliding door to the balcony. She needs to sleep downstairs with you. These things are not safe."

"O-Okay..."

Ash let go of me and walked out of the kitchen, taking the stairs two at a time up to his room. I didn't end up making breakfast, choosing to fix myself a mimosa instead. I continued to stare out the window for a while, though all I saw were squirrels and deer.

Moss and Ben were the next to wake up and stumble into the kitchen. They walked right by me with a bleary-eyed nod and Ben grabbed three beers out of the fridge, handing one to me. We drank in silence for a minute while I tried to decide the best way to tell them about Ash. Just as I was contemplating telling them at all, Mel bounded into the room and took stock of the three of us as we all froze mid-gulp. She tsk-tsked.

"Look at all these beer bottles littered around the cabin. Are you guys planning to clean up your empties?"

Moss, Ben and I exchanged a glance. Ben was the first to lower his beer.

"Oh, don't mind these fallen soldiers," he said, bring a trash can to the edge of the counter and sweeping a group of empty bottles into it. "Thank you for your service, boys."

Moss and I lowered our drinks and saluted the bottles as they clanged to the bottom of the trash can.

"Oh, you three are ridiculous. And probably alcoholics." Mel laughed and shook a righteous finger at us.

"No probably about it."

"Cheers to that."

"Well, it's easier to do Lloyd's mom when I'm drunk."

Lloyd walked into the kitchen just then and threw Moss such a rage-filled look that I involuntarily took a step away from him.

"M- Morning babe..." I tried.

Lloyd grabbed the nearby empty orange juice bottle from the counter and threw it into the trash. Saying nothing to anyone, he stalked back to his room just as Ash came down the stairs. He was pulling on his jacket and adjusting the beanie on the top of his head.

"Hey, where you goin', man?" Ben asked.

"To the nearest cabin I can find."

"Wait, babe!" Mel ran over to him as Ash turned away from us and threw open the front door. "Why? Do you want me to go with you?"

"To find more ammunition. I didn't bring enough."

"Enough for what...." Moss asked slowly.

"For them. They're getting closer to the house. They've started coming out in the day now, too."

"What?"

"Who is, babe?"

Ben and I exchanged a glance over a confused Moss and Mel.

"Ashley." Ben said soberly. "If someone is stalking us, let's just leave right now. Why bother with ammunition?"

Ash laughed as if it were the most ridiculous thing he'd ever heard. "We can't leave. They've already disabled all the vehicles."

"They *what?*"

"Of course they did." Ash said, incredulously.

"We'll call for a tow then."

"Yeah, on what? When is the last time any of you saw your phones?"

I glanced around the room. *Not since yesterday.*

"Look, just stay in the house," Ash ordered. "I'll be gone five hours at the most. No one leaves, no matter what you see outside. They'll probably be more brazen once I'm gone. Got it?"

"Ashley..." Mel whispered, uneasily.

"Just...*sigh*...just stay here, Mel, please. I can't protect any of you if you go outside." Ash walked over and hugged Mel tightly, kissing the top of her head.

"Ash, let me go with you." Ben said.

"Yeah, please take someone with you." I agreed.

Ash let go of Mel and walked out the door without saying another word to anyone.

*

We spent the rest of the morning trying to find our phones, connect our laptops to wifi and start our cars. When all of that failed, we tried to drink our worries away while Mel sat on the loveseat and stared out the window arranging her gentle features to an impassive, stony expression. And when the rain set in around 1, and the thunder began to shake the house, we stopped drinking and started pacing.

Lloyd - still deeply focused on his book - wouldn't unlock the door or speak to anyone until the rain started. At that point Ben and I sat everyone down and told them we knew of Ash's current state of mind. The five of us stood in my bedroom leaning against the wall and rubbing our faces in stress and exhaustion.

"Why the fuck did you guys let him leave?" Lloyd asked over and over again.

"I don't know!" Melanie cried. "I didn't want him to; I tried to go with him!"

"I'm talking to these three drunk idiots over here."

Ben opened his mouth to object but I beat him to it.

"We're on fucking vacation, Lloyd, that's why we're drinking and hanging out while *you're* sitting behind a closed door working on some fucking book I've never heard of."

"All you guys have done is get drunk for the last three fucking days."

"Well, at least we've been doing *some*thing!"

"Alright, alright." Lloyd relented. "Let's just figure out what we're going to do."

"I'm going upstairs to lay down." Melanie said, flatly. "Wake me up when Ashley gets back."

"Mel-" started Ben.

"Please." She held up a hand, "I can't. I just need to lay down for a while.

As soon as Mel walked out the door, Moss turned to us with a whisper.

"Guys, it's now been 5 and a half hours since Ash left. He said 5 hours at most. I think we should go look for him."

"No!" Ben said quickly. "We can't leave the house. That's the last thing Ash said before he left."

"Ash isn't thinking clearly," I interjected. "He may be hurt or lost or both. We need to go find him."

"Does he have his phone?" Lloyd asked.

"No one has their phones." Ben's voice was impassive.

As Lloyd listened to Moss and Ben make their arguments for going after Ash or listening to his warning, I stared out the window at the trees Ash had been watching earlier. Movement had caught my eye beyond the tree line and I was desperately trying to find what was out there. But, in the darkened, stormy sky, the task was almost impossible. I listened absentmindedly as I searched.

Lloyd: "What made him think there were any cabins nearby?"

Moss: "I figured he saw one on the way in."

Lloyd: "And what made him think those cabins had spare ammo?"

Moss: "I think that was a gamble on his part."

Lloyd: "So then he must have seen something that really freaked him out."

Ben: "He did."

Lloyd: "Then, what, he disabled all the cars himself? And stashed the phones somewhere?"

Ben: "This is really not good, guys."

Moss: "Look he's our friend and he needs help. Whatever he's doing, you know he doesn't realize he's doing it."

There! There it was. In the trees. Something was high in the trees, hanging on one branch from their arms and standing on the one below it facing the cabin. There was no way it was an animal; even in the dark and the distance I could tell it was human. Just as I was about to point it out to Lloyd, lightning flashed and my night vision disappeared. I would have looked for the figure again but something else had caught my eye in the half second of light. Something that was in front of the house that shouldn't be there.

Without saying a word, I walked out of the room and down the hall to the living room. Though the sky was dark and the light was minimal, there was no denying what was waiting out there in the darkness.

The boys had followed me out of the room with questions but when they saw what I was looking at the cabin went silent. "What the fuck..."

Moss gave a nervous laugh. "He's fucking with us. That's Ash fucking with us. It has to be."

"I don't think so," Ben whispered.

Through the sheets of rain and the encroaching fog on the mountain there had appeared a fresh mound of dirt the size of a person and a jagged rock from the wood to serve as a tombstone.

I tore my eyes from the macabre scene in front of me and Lloyd suddenly grabbed Moss and pinned him up against the wall. I hadn't heard what was said, but Lloyd was suddenly very pissed off.

"Is that another fucking joke about my mother, Moss?!"

"No! No man, I was just saying-"

"I've had enough of your goddamn shit. If you ever-"

"Lloyd," I screamed at him, "Let go of him. Since when do you give a wet fuck about Moss's jokes? Don't you think we have bigger problems?"

"Stay the fuck out of this, Ingrid."

I looked to Ben for help but he was still staring at the grave outside.

A creak of old wood behind us broke the spell and we all turned to see Mel coming down the stairs.

"Why are you guys yelling?"

I took a step toward her like I was trying to corner a frightened animal. "Mel..."

"Has Ashley- what the fuck is that?"

Lloyd let go of Moss and took a step toward Melanie's other side. "Mel."

Mel stumbled on a stair but caught herself. "Is that a fucking grave?"

"Mel, relax, it's just Ash fucking with us," said Moss.

"Shut up, Moss, Ash didn't do this." Ben snapped.

"Is that a fucking *grave?*" Mel yelled and bolted for the sliding glass door to the deck.

"Mel, wait!"

She slid the door open and was about to run out into the rain when Ben caught her around the waist. "You can't go out there!" He yelled.

Mel suddenly collapsed in a pile of tears and screaming.

"It's him! It's Ashley, he's dead! Oh my God, Ashley no, fuck, who did that. Who put him in there? Ashley..."

Ben deposited Mel on the loveseat and Lloyd closed the door. Mel buried herself in the cushions and sobbed.

"If it is Ash in that grave," Lloyd whispered to us. "Then who buried him?"

"Ask Ben." I shot Ben a questioning look. It was clear he knew more about the situation than even I did.

He returned my look with one of warning.

"I know you saw something, too, Ben."

"Well, what did *you* see, Ingrid?" Moss asked.

"I- I saw someone in a tree. I think. They were hanging from one of the branches at the top."

"Yeah," Ben sighed. "I've seen them, too."

"Them?" Lloyd raised an eyebrow.

"Or 'it', rather. It's not a person."

"Well, then what is it?"

"It's...hard to describe."

"Wait!" I ran into the kitchen and grabbed Ash's drawing off the counter.

"Did it look like this?" I held the paper out to Ben.

"Yes. Sort of. I mean I think so, I didn't see it that well."

Moss laughed. "That's a stick figure. Big round head, lines for body and limbs... That's a kid's drawing."

"No," I said, "It's Ashes depiction of what is out there, this is what he thought he was seeing. Look, if it's Ash or somebody else - and fuck, I pray that it's Ash - I agree with Ben that it's not safe. Maybe they're just trying to scare us but either way, we can't leave this cabin."

"Somebody go help Ashley..." Mel moaned from behind us.

Lloyd shook his head and gave her a gentle look. "There's nothing we can do right now, Mel." His voice shook.

The rain let up as the sun set that night, though we had already been under darkness for hours from the storm. We'd agreed that Moss and Mel would sleep on the 2nd floor - the main floor - with everyone else. We also decided to rotate sentry shifts all night so that someone was always awake waiting for

Ash and watching for the figure in the woods. All except Mel, who was an inconsolable mess. She was the first to pass out.

I conversed quietly with Lloyd until Moss and Ben went to Ben's room down the hall to sleep.

"I don't want to sleep, Lloyd. I can't." I whispered in the darkness.

"You need to try. Your shift isn't until 4am."

"I don't want to sleep in the back bedroom alone."

"Then you shouldn't. Go get the quilts and pillows and sleep out here next to Mel." He yawned.

"It's freezing out here."

"I know, Ing, I'll go down to the basement and throw some more wood in the furnace. I would have done it earlier but...that room freaks me out."

"I haven't been down there yet but everything about this cabin freaks me out. Are you gonna be able to stay awake until Moss's shift?"

"Yeah, I'm going to write." Lloyd pointed to his laptop on the couch.

I gathered up 2 quilts and a pillow from our room and left the rest of the bedding for Lloyd. Even though I didn't feel at all tired I fell into a dreamless asleep almost immediately. I woke up just as the first rays of sunlight were drawing the darkness from the room. I shot up when I realized I must have missed my shift.

Mel was still sleeping next to me, shaking in the cold of the morning. It was clear Lloyd had never put more wood in the furnace. There was no one else in the room.

"Lloyd?" I yelled down the hall. He didn't answer.

"Lloyd!" I yelled louder and got to my feet, dropping my quilts over Melanie.

A door opened and a red-eyed Ben stumbled out. "What's wrong?"

"I slept through my shift. Did you?"

"Yeah...I think Moss took them all. Is he not out there?"

"No. Is he not in there?"

"No."

We both turned our heads at the same time to look down the hall at Lloyd's door. The implication was sobering. Ben turned back and gave me a nod that acted more as an agreement between us. He walked down the corridor to check on Lloyd and I drew a deep ragged breath before I turned around to do my part.

And it was there, the thing I hadn't wanted to see. A second grave had appeared next to the first; with another giant rock to serve as tombstone.

"Ben..."

*

"We have to wake her up soon." I looked over at Mel as I sat on the couch absentmindedly folding and unfolding Ash's drawing over and over.

"Not yet." Lloyd stared through the window at the rain and smoked out of cracked sliding door.

"So...he didn't say anything to you? Did he tell you he was planning to go outside?" I asked.

"He didn't say anything to me. I woke Moss up, told him it was his turn, he nodded and then got up and I went to bed."

"We told him to stay in the cabin," Ben muttered, shaking his head. "It's not safe out there. They're out there."

"What are they?" I asked.

"Does it matter?" Ben didn't spare me a look.

Lloyd flicked his cigarette outside and slid the door shut. "Not anymore. This is only a game of survival now."

"Yes it does matter," I countered. "Part of surviving is knowing how to defend ourselves."

"Then we do what Ash told us to do and stay in the cabin until someone comes looking for us." Ben said.

"And if Ash is the one doing this?" I shot back.

"It's NOT Ash."

Mel continued to sleep while we argued quietly with one another. The rain from the day before had left the mountain cloudy and soaked in mist. The graves were thankfully concealed by a thick, gray fog by the time Mel woke up.

The entire morning something had been bothering me about the room we were standing in. Something was not right, something had changed. I could see it there out of the corner of my eye. But every time I turned to look nothing was out of place. It distressed me to the point that I brought it up to Ben and Lloyd.

"Do you guys notice anything...I don't know, different around here?"

"Yeah. There are graves in the front yard."

"No, Lloyd, I mean different about this room. Something is bothering me..."

I followed my peripheral vision around the room again but nothing popped out at me.

"No, Ingrid. Right now we're trying to figure out how best to survive *out*side of the house."

"Wait, we- we're leaving the cabin?" I sputtered.

"Lloyd thinks we should," answered Ben.

"What, no, why the fuck would we do that?!"

After continuing to argue for hours with Ben and Lloyd about the best course of action we decided that, in the absence of phones and neighbors, the two of them would have to try to fix one of the cars with their limited knowledge of mechanics. Since Lloyd's jeep was the oldest - and therefore, they reasoned, the most mechanically simple - they decided to work on that car first.

I was to stand guard on the overlooking deck and watch anything that moved. Ash had taken his gun with him when he left the day before, but we reasoned a warning was better than nothing at all.

Mel spent most of the morning sitting on the deck with me watching the trees through the fog. I don't know when she noticed the absence of Moss and the appearance of the second grave but she didn't mentioned it.

The boys had only been out there an hour when I heard a loud thud from above us. It had come from the roof.

"Mel, did you hear that?" I whispered.

She nodded but continued her vigil over the wood. I leaned over the railing and yelled down at Ben, who was sitting in the front seat of the car keying the ignition.

"I'll be right back. Mel will watch you guys."

Ben nodded but Lloyd had his head buried in the engine which was desperately trying to turn over. Mel turned her head to look down at them but otherwise seemed uninvested.

"If you see anything, yell out, ok?"

Mel gave an almost imperceptible nod.

"I mean it, Mel, anything."

"Yep."

Having no plan at all except to hope I'd hear the thud again, I went inside and climbed the stairs to Mel and Ash's room on the 3rd floor. I stood there quietly for what seemed like ages with only the sound of the jeep turning over to pierce through the silence of the mountain. Finally, I went to the sliding door to look at the tree line of the forest, which was now almost impossible to see through the heavy fog.

And then I heard it again. But it wasn't a thud...it was footstep. My breath caught in my throat. And then another step. Someone was walking on the roof directly above me. They were slow, heavy, careful footsteps.

On blind, dumb instinct I ripped open the sliding door to the balcony. Just as I took a step out, an earsplitting scream sliced through the chill, outside air.

Lloyd.

I spun away from the door and ran down the stairs as fast as I could, falling once on the landing. I jerked on the front door to run outside but it wouldn't budge. In desperation, I ran out onto the deck to find Mel where I'd left her - completely unaware and again staring at the trees.

I ran to the railing and saw the thing; it was running towards a copse of trees and dragging something behind it. It was too tall to be Ben or Lloyd. I screamed for Melanie and she instantly snapped out of her spell.

"Wha- what happened?"

"Goddamn it, Mel!" I cried. She followed me inside and I again tried the front door, screaming for Ben and Lloyd in blind panic.

"Ingrid?" I heard a voice echo up the basement stairs.

"Ben!" My voice broke over his name.

I ran down the basement stairs skipping two or three steps at a time as Mel hurried behind. When I reached the bottom, Ben was standing in the doorway of the basement bedroom holding a small, black box.

"Ben, where's Lloyd?" I choked out as soon as I saw him.

"What?"

"Where the fuck is Lloyd?"

Ben looked perplexed and nodded at the open door I hadn't noticed before. "He's still out with the car, wh- why aren't you guys watching him?"

"He's not there," I shook my head in shock and tears spilled down my cheeks. "I heard him scream and I just saw someone running away from the jeep."

The small box fell from Ben's hands and crashed to the floor, assorted tools fanning out in every direction. I made for the door but Ben caught me in one arm and slammed the door shut with the other.

"No, Ingrid. Don't."

I thrashed against him ineffectively until I melted into a hysterical pile of broken girl at his feet. Ben sat down on the floor next to me and held me while I convulsed in sobs. Mel watched the scene for a moment and then slid down the side of the old, metal furnace to rest her back against it and silently cry.

I don't know how long we sat there but it felt like only minutes. The tears hadn't even dried from my face when we heard a door creak open upstairs. I knew immediately it was the jammed front door.

Mel's eyes widened and Ben slowly let go of me and stood up. He put a finger to his lips and began quietly climbing the stairs - we'd left the basement door open.

Mel and I barely breathed as we heard Ben's footfalls reach the landing. Suddenly there was the sound of heavy, hurried footsteps running across the floor above us. We heard Ben run up the rest of the way to the door and slam it shut. Then silence. Mel and I got to our feet.

Ben descended back down to the basement and by the time he got to the bottom his face had drained of color and his body was wracked with shudders.

"Who was it, Ben?"

"Was it Ashley?"

Ben shook his head and ran a trembling hand through his hair. "The- the door locks from this side. We should be safe." But I didn't think a locked door was going to stop it.

We sat Ben down and Mel held him while I paced around the room. There was no more sound from above but that meant we hadn't heard the thing leave, either. I paced the basement floor staring out the window as I passed by it until the fog momentarily cleared and I saw the thing I'd been dreading - the third grave. Lloyd's grave. I grabbed onto the window ledge as my legs gave out beneath me. I tried to recover quickly, for Mel's sake. The girl was barely holding it together.

"What? What is it?" Mel asked.

"Nothing. It's nothing; I just haven't eaten since yesterday."

Ben gave me a look that said he knew what I'd seen and Mel sprang up to run to the window since she wasn't buying it either.

"No..." Mel whispered and her voice cracked. "No! We have to find Ashley. He can stop all this!"

Before I could grab her, Mel was on the staircase, taking them two at a time.

"Mel!" I screamed at her.

"What if that was Ashley up there? What if he's come back for us?"

Melanie, being the gentle soul that she was, just wasn't prepared to handle any more of it. She was out of her mind in grief and fear.

By the time I caught up with her, Mel had already thrown open the basement door and stepped out into the living room area. There was nothing there. I entered the room cautiously behind her and immediately noticed that whatever had been bothering me that morning was still there and that the uneasy feeling it gave me was more pronounced than ever.

"Melanie..." I breathed. "We have to get out of here."

I stepped toward her to drag her back down the stairs but she bolted for the front door which was still standing open. I took one last long look around the room and ran out the door and down the stairs after Mel.

By the time I reached the ground, Ben had already thrown open the basement door and was ahead of me in the chase. By the time he reached her, Mel was tearing through the wet soil of the first grave plot – Ash's grave – with her bare hands.

Ben grabbed her shoulders to pull her away and then suddenly froze. I came up next to him and watched as Mel tore through the mud and dirt for an eternity until she finally hit packed earth.

"It's empty." She looked up at us with mud and tears dripping down her face. "Ashley isn't dead!"

"Ash is alive..." I breathed. "Are- are all of these graves empty?"

I walked over to the grave that would have been Lloyd's and began scraping away the loose earth. It was much easier to dig up than the first plot because the grave was fresh and the dirt was dry. Mel sat back on her haunches and watched me hopefully as Ben stared out ahead of us.

"Guys..."

"Ben, fucking help me."

"Guys, we have to go. Now." Ben said without looking away from the trees.

"But Lloyd-"

My fingers caught on something hard deep in dirt. And I didn't have to know much to know I was suddenly holding a rib cage. I jerked my hand out in horror.

"Jesus fuck!"

I fell back on my hands and scooted away from the hole in revulsion.

Mel shook her head in disbelief. "But..."

"Then it's Ash!" I screamed at her. "It's Ash who's doing this! He's killing everyone, he killed Lloyd!"

Mel shook her head fervently and stood up to walk over to me. "How-"

"He's been murdering us, Melanie, don't you get it? His mind is fucked. He killed Moss and he killed Lloyd and he'll kill you too. He's out there right now-"

SLAP

Melanie pulled her hand back and cradled it to her breast. "How dare you. How dare you?! You're supposed to be his friend, Ingrid, you've known him all your life. Ashley didn't do this. Ashley would never hurt the people he loved! He'd never hurt me!"

I cupped my cheek with the hand that had so recently held Lloyd's bones. "There is no other possibility, Melanie." I said, icily.

She took a step away from me, and opened her mouth but it fell into a gape and her face suddenly went white. Mel stumbled and fell to the ground but was back on her feet in an instant. She looked up at the house and then back down at me.

"He deserved better from his friends, Ingrid." Mel's voice cracked and then she turned and fled for the tree line.

"Ben!" I screamed, "Stop her!" But Ben was already moving toward me at lightning speed. He grabbed my arm and pulled me to my feet and back toward the cabin.

"Ben!" I screamed. "We have to get Mel!"

"Mel is gone, we can't help her now."

As soon as the door to the cabin closed behind us, I ripped off my mud caked jacket and threw it at Ben.

"What the fuck is wrong with you?"

"They were there. They were out there."

"There is no 'they', Ben. There's only Ash."

"No, Ash is dead; he was probably killed minutes after walking out of this cabin."

"Then where's his body, Ben? Why is his grave empty?"

I knew I was starting to snap. The shock, the absurdity of it all...my brain couldn't comprehend what was happening to me anymore.

"I don't know. It was the first grave; it was made to- made to draw us out there."

"By Ash. There's no other logical-"

"No!" Ben shook his head. "Mel was right, Ash wouldn't do that."

"Well he did do that."

"You're wrong."

"Because there's no other alternative-"

"Those things we're seeing aren't Ash!"

"-and I refuse to believe that stick figure people-"

"You have to accept the fact-"

"-are running around the woods killing our friends-"

"-that we're being hunted out here-"

"- and field-stripping their dead bodies!"

"-by something fucked up and inhuman!"

"-when it's clearly Ashley suffering from some sort of PTSD!"

"It's not Ash, Ingrid."

"He murdered Lloyd!"

"Listen to me-"

"Ashley fucking murdered Lloyd!"

"No-"

"There's no-"

"I did it! Okay? I killed Lloyd."

I shook my head, disoriented and took a step backward.

"It was me, Ingrid! I killed him." Ben's voice broke over my name.

"Why are you saying that...?" I choked.

"Because it's true. Out by the jeep-"

"Stop."

"And I'm pretty sure that Lloyd ki-"

"Stop!"

"Ingrid, you have to listen to me if you want to survive. Those things, they have this power - when they're near you - to make you so angry. Fuck, I mean, fuck, I just, I couldn't stop hitting Lloyd's-"

"STOP!" I gasped, trying desperately to draw air into my lungs. I clutched the back of the couch for support. I could feel a blind, foreign rage building in me and I turned my knuckles white trying to quell it.

"Are you on Ash's side?" I whispered, finally. "Did he tell you to hurt Lloyd?"

"No, I just...I just killed him."

"And who peeled the flesh from his bones and buried him in the ground then, Benjamin?" I said and was unsettled by the flat, impassive tone of my voice.

"They did."

"Why would they do that?"

Ben nodded to Lloyd's computer, which was sitting open on the coffee table where he'd left after he went to bed at the end of his watch.

"Read what Lloyd has been writing, Ingrid."

Keeping a wary eye on Ben I rounded the couch and picked up the computer, waking up the monitor with a swipe of my finger.

There were only 15 pages - which didn't seem like much for the days he'd spent locked away writing - and while it started out like any other story, the text quickly descended into nonsense and random strings of alphanumeric until the last three pages on which he'd simply typed *It Eats Us* over and over again.

I slammed the laptop shut and threw it across the floor. Then I walked over to fridge, pulled out the last beer in it - one of Ben's- and dropped down into the nearest chair.

Ben hadn't moved.

"I'm so sorry, Ingrid. I'm so sorry. I loved Lloyd like a brother and I just snapped. I was just standing there holding the crowbar and thinking about-"

"Stop talking, Ben."

He stopped but choked on a sob in his throat. Ben was right. Mel was right. It wasn't Ash, it couldn't be. It was something else altogether, something that lived out in the wood.

"Ingrid, I have to-"

"Ben, the only reason you're telling me this is because they want you to, I'd guess. I don't have a reason to hate you and so they're allowing you to give me one."

CREAK

Ben and I looked at each other and then at the door to the basement. It was coming up the stairs.

I knew it was over, we were totally fucked. There was nothing left to do but die. I raised my beer to Ben, gave him a solemn nod, took a long gulp and then hurled the bottle at the basement door where is shattered against the wood.

"Fuck you!" I screamed at the thing.

"Ingrid," Ben brought my attention back to him and he looked at me pleadingly, through the veil of a thousand different emotions. "Run."

Before I could respond, Ben dove for the basement door and threw himself down the stairs. I shot up out of the chair in horror as his body made the most tortured and sickening screams I had ever heard.

I stood there for long seconds listening to his flesh ripping apart against the soundtrack of a low, satisfied growl.

I was frozen. I was alone. And as I looked desperately around the room for something to fight with, I found the thing that I couldn't see before, the thing that had bothered me about the room since Moss's disappearance.

And it wasn't frightening or even unsettling; it was just...out of place.

There had appeared sometime overnight a very long, very thin black line that ran vertically on the wall from the floor to almost the ceiling. It was hard to see and at first glance it appeared to be a crack in the wood but when I really looked at it, it somehow wasn't actually the wall at all.

And then, as I was studying it, it moved and expanded to become the tall, black stick man from Ash's drawing. No, it hadn't expanded...it had turned toward me. The thing was as thin as a few pieces of construction paper.

I can tell you that when you're presented with something so impossible and something so innately wrong, you don't scream. You don't gasp. You just stand there frozen with confusion and, in my case, crippling fear.

It took another creak from the basement stairs to snap me out of my catatonia. The creature that had been quietly standing in front of me suddenly sprang to life and ran at me with all the fluidity of an animated drawing.

Since it was between me and front door I turned and fled out onto the deck through the sliding glass door which Mel had left blessedly open. I ran to the end of the patio, and without taking half a second to think, climbed over the wooden railing and jumped off.

I heard the bones break underneath me when I landed but adrenaline kept the pain from crippling me entirely. I ran as best I could across the clearing toward the tree line. As I ran the fog thinned and I saw the third stick man waiting for me in the trees.

I quickly tried to change course and fell on my broken ankles. When I looked up to see if it was coming toward me, I saw that it wasn't actually a stick man at all, it was something almost worse. It was Melanie.

She was hanging by the neck from a tree branch, facing the cabin and, consequently, me. I was on my feet and running toward her in under a second. When I got to her I could tell immediately that I was far too late to be of any help to her and far too short to get her down. All I could do was watch her dead body swing in the wind and cry. I wondered where the rope had come from.

I looked back at the house then, to see if the stick men were close, but it wasn't them that I noticed. It was what Melanie had seen out at the graves, the thing that had made her run.

Ash was on the roof, lying there, splayed out for us all to see. His head was untouched and his mouth has fallen open into a long O. His hands and shoes were pristine, too. But the rest of his body; from his neck, to his wrists, to his ankles were picked clean of flesh. He was simply a brittle skeleton with a face.

So, they had done this. They had done this to Ash and they had done this to Mel, gave her the tools she needed to die. And soon she would look just like Ash did. I couldn't bear the thought.

I tried everything I could think of to get her down from the high branch until the physical pain ebbed in and, just as it did, I saw the shape of a stick man walking toward me through the fog. I told Melanie's body I was sorry and then I ran, falling only once as I sprinted away from the horrors of the mountain.

The Stick Man never caught me because it didn't want to. After hours of walking, when I thought the agony of my broken bones and soul was going to kill me, I could still see them in the wood. And Ash was right, there were three. They would appear as a silhouette and then disappear as they turned to walk and reappear...well, anywhere. But they would always turn up closer to me than they were before.

And then, long after night had fallen, I tripped on a dirt road and didn't get back up. I stared up at an empty, starless sky and waited for a passerby or a Stick Man to claim me. It was a young mother and her son, in the end.

No one ever believed me about the Stick Men.

They told me all of our phones were found in our rooms. They said there was nothing wrong with the cars. That may be true now, but it wasn't then. I know they'll never believe me about what really happened out in the woods, but I'll always know. The Stick Men stripped our souls away. And then the Stick Men ate what was left.

DOLLHOUSE

I grew up in Keeling, Missouri. No, you wouldn't have heard of it. It was a small, rural, lower-middle class community where everyone owned an acre or two. My father was a writer and my mother wanted to keep horses so Keeling was the perfect little "one stoplight town" for them to settle in and raise children.

We lived there until suddenly, in 1984, the government claimed eminent domain on all of Keeling and we were bought out. My dad decided to move us to sunny California.

I'm a writer, too, though I'm not as well-known as my father. I write informational pieces for online magazines and blogs. And of course that means I'm barely getting by. So when one of my editors asked me to write an article on eminent domain for a popular political website, I jumped at the chance. She told me she chosen me because I had first-hand experience with eminent domain and the buyer wanted an Op-Ed piece that included photos.

I packed my bags for the following week, excited for the project. I'd always been curious about what became of my hometown, anyway. Before he died, my dad told me he thought Keeling had been turned into a small airport.

First: research. I was disappointed to find the internet all but mute on the old town - citing my sources was going to be difficult. I knew Keeling had been near Poplar Bluff, Missouri so I pulled up Google Earth and followed the 67 north to the turn off for Keeling.

Odd. The entire town was...blank. Not blank like there weren't any buildings, blank like there was a gaping black hole where Keeling was - an omission in the satellite data. It could only mean one thing. I slammed my laptop shut and threw the mouse against the wall. It was private - and likely classified - government land now.

I hemmed and hawed about it a few days before deciding to go anyway. This particular buyer had allotted me a per diem (funds) for travel and I thought I might as well use them. Maybe there was still a story here.

Two days later I was driving through Poplar Bluff in a rented Ford Focus. I stopped at a gas station for some water and granola bars, deciding to check into the hotel after I got back from Keeling. I was looking forward to seeing it again.

I took the exit for North 67 and drove until I realized I'd missed the turn off. I circled back, looking for anything familiar. I had to drive back and forth a few times before I found it. Barely there, covered in plant life and completely unrecognizable, was a road. I'd seen this street a million times, but never unpaved which is why I'd missed it. Someone had pulled up the asphalt and the road was completely overgrown. Bizarre.

I drove the six miles into Keeling wishing I had rented something with bigger tires and a higher clearance. On the last mile the pavement returned and I rolled into the abandoned business district of Keeling. It was small: a post office, a gas station and a bar. All the buildings were derelict and rotting, their decay far more consistent with something left sitting for 100 years - not 30.

I drove through the eerily quiet town with the burned out stoplight and continued down route 51 toward my old house.

As I passed the other houses on the street, I noticed they were in the same state of advanced decay as the buildings in town. It was unsettling, pulling up to the house I'd lived in only 30 years before to find it crumbling and consumed by time.

I went through every room in my house for the nostalgia, but found nothing of interest. We had packed well - there was nothing left here but a sheet-covered mannequin my mom's sewing room and rotting moving boxes on the floor.

I left my old house and continued down the road, which by now had turned back to dirt. Just why had the government bought this place? Why spend all that money, buy up all this land and then abandon it? My stomach knotted as I started to realize there may be a very big story here. I was not going to return to LA empty handed.

I counted house after house knowing I was reaching the end of the street. All were in varied states of decomposition, some had even collapsed in on themselves.

The house at the end of the drive began coming in to view. I slowed down to take it in as it filled my windshield. I never remembered this particular house being enormous, but then, memories of children were often distorted one way or another.

While every other building in Keeling was disintegrating this house stood proud and palatial, untouched by the decades. It was almost as if the house at the end of the drive was stealing the energy, life even, of every other building in town. And maybe even more than that.

An expansive, very clear and defined area of dead grass encircled the house. Two dead trees stood skeletized within its radius. Toxic ground water, perhaps? The windows were all barred, save a small, circular port window on the third story. If the government had claimed this town for any particular reason, could it be this house? Was this what they were hiding? Was this my story? I couldn't remember anyone ever living here and the house was so different from the others. I had to know why.

Smelling a story at last, I parked in the pristine white driveway and climbed out of my car, hauling my camera and laptop cases over my shoulder. I walked up the four steps to the door and was delighted to find it unlocked.

The foyer was large and made almost entirely of marble, save a large mirror. The house had a delightful Baroque theme to it, and all the beautiful, ornate fixtures shined as if they'd just been polished. A staircase to the second floor was set right in front of me, a floor to ceiling mirror on the wall to my left and a closed door and hallway beyond it on my right. I set my stuff down and took my phone out - no signal. *Fantastic.* Looks like I wouldn't be calling the hotel about my late arrival.

I toured the house, snapping a few pictures with my cell as I walked. The first floor had a library, a living room, a kitchen and a dining room. All the furniture had been left behind, even the dining room table was set. Everything was orderly and oddly dust free. Was someone still living here?

The second floor had 4 bedrooms and another narrow staircase that led up to the attic. I tried the attic door first, but it was locked. The first room I entered was the master bedroom. It was simple and cozy unlike the rest of the house and it had an adjoining bathroom. I eyed the bed with interest, a sudden idea coming to me. I may not have to leave Keeling tonight after all.

The next room over from the master stood with door ajar. This room was bare except for nine mannequins, all covered in musty, yellowed sheets like the one at my house. I snapped a quick picture and left, closing the door to the room.

The next door in the hallway was closed. I opened it and cringed: this room had a child's bed and was filled wall to wall with dolls.

I circled the room, curiously picking up a few. Baby Alive dolls, Cabbage patch dolls, and tons of creepy, little, yellowing porcelain dolls. They had all been positioned to be looking at the bed. I snapped two pictures in this room vowing to come back with my Canon.

I closed this door too and entered the last room on the second floor. It was a simple office - green carpet and green wallpaper. It had a plain desk and tan typewriter with a new white - not yellowed - piece of paper loaded into it. Interesting.

I left this room and descended the stairs. It was time to bring out the big guns. I bent down to unsheathe my Canon when movement caught my eye to my right. I turned and looked into the mirror. I'd known it was there subconsciously so what had caught my attention? I reached for my camera again and realized what was wrong.

The mirror, more specifically my movements in it, were almost imperceptibly out of sync. When I moved my arm, my reflection did so about a quarter second later. When I blinked, my eyes were still closed in the mirror when I opened them again. It was completely unsettling and I could feel my skin crawl.

I continued to watch my delayed reflection when I suddenly heard a noise like the creaking of wood, perhaps a stair. But it didn't come from the staircase on the right, it came from directly behind me, behind the basement door. Someone was coming up the stairs of the basement. So there was someone here! I dubiously gripped the basement door and tried to open it but - like the attic - it was locked. I knocked on the door but heard only silence below. An animal perhaps?

Still determined to find my story I opened the front door to unload my car and almost fell over. *What the....* My car, which I had definitely parked at the top of the driveway, was now parked at the bottom of the driveway, almost in the street. I had parked it at the top of the driveway, hadn't I? I'd just been so excited...I couldn't remember. Had I not put the parking brake on? Had it rolled backwards?

I unloaded the car and brought my stuff up to the master bedroom. As I walked by the sewing room I noticed the door stood open again - but I knew I had closed it. I peered in and this time I counted 14 sheeted mannequins in it. There had been only 9 just a few minutes ago. Right? Something was definitely going on. I mused that perhaps it was all in my head. Maybe the air was toxic, poisonous and that's why the government pushed everyone out of Keeling. Was I losing it? I took another photo.

By the time I had deposited everything in the master bedroom, I was winded. I felt so weak and so exhausted that I had to rest on the bed for just a moment. I laid worrying that many the weakness and hallucinations were a sign to get the hell out of Keeling.

I must have fallen asleep because the next I know I was awoken by a high, small voice. "Say bye-bye!"

I bolted upright and looked around in a panic, eventually noticing one of the dolls from the little girl's room sitting on the bedside table. It was one of the shudder-inducing small, porcelain ones.

I rubbed my eyes and glanced around the room. I jumped when in the muted light of the setting sun I saw someone in the corner. Wait, not someone...something. It was one of those stupid sheet-covered mannequins. I blinked several times. That definitely wasn't there before.

I got out of bed and walked over to stare at it. Someone was fucking with me, I knew it. I started to raise the sheet to see underneath when I heard a loud bang from downstairs. I let the sheet drop and started toward the bedroom door when I suddenly felt very sick. I dashed into the bathroom and threw up in the toilet. It wasn't safe here, I definitely needed to leave. I knew I didn't have a lot of time left to investigate.

I got up from the toilet and splashed water on my face. This time when I looked into the bathroom mirror my reflection's movements were at least a half second behind mine. I waved my hands in front of the mirror horrified by my reflection's slow response. I watched the blood leave my face and gaped at my reflection in dismay. How was this even possible?

Of course, it wasn't. This didn't feel like a hallucination. Maybe I wasn't breathing in toxic air at all. Was all this supernatural? Possibly. I mean, what scientific explanations were there? I'd wanted a story and I'd gotten one. I could be the first journalist to prove the existence of...what? Ghosts? Demons? Poltergeists? I guess it didn't matter. It was my payday - and I was going to need evidence.

As I turned away from the mirror to find my camera, I could have sworn I saw my reflection wink at me. I grabbed the Canon off the floor and began photographing everything I saw. I went downstairs to re-shoot every room, starting with the library. I started pulling books out one by one and saw that that every single book in the library was a version of the Christian Bible. Different versions in different languages. I opened a few that were in English and found that the word 'God' was scratched out on every page, in every book.

It was getting dark and just as I thought about trying to flip the circuit breaker a lamp flicked on in the dining room pouring light out into the hallway. I tried to get ahold of myself and quiet my shaking hands.

I turned my camera to photograph the corridor when I suddenly heard heavy stomping. It was more than stomping, it was almost running - and the sound was coming down the hallway right towards me. I dropped the camera and stood frozen with fear.

Whatever it was entered the library and stomped right up in front of me. I couldn't see anything, but there was definitely something there - I could feel it blocking me from leaving. I slowly pulled my phone out of my pocket and took a picture of whatever was right in front of my face. The flash momentarily blinded me and when I recovered my vision, all the books in the library were on the floor, as if they had been ripped from the shelves in a rage, and in only that few seconds of silence. But I felt that whatever had been standing in front of me was gone.

I picked up the Canon, took a few more shaky pictures, and tiptoed my way out of the room. I realized that what I really needed was video. I pulled my cell phone out again and opened it up to video recording then walked down the hallway toward the lit dining room. I passed a painting in the hallway and caught sight of my smirking reflection. But I wasn't smiling.

As soon as I entered the dining room, I noticed something was different. A noose made of stained sheets was now tied to a beam above the table. It was swinging back and forth as if it were weighted, but nothing else in the room was moving. Even the beamed creaked as it swung, as if it, too, was straining from the weight of something. I filmed it for a minute and then raised the Canon for a picture. It suddenly stopped swinging as if someone had grabbed it midair. I heard giggling from upstairs.

I left the dining room and walked warily toward the staircase. Did I really want to go up there? The giggling was gone but I could hear the typewriter clicking away. I happened to glance toward the large foyer mirror again to see it was now out of sync a full second behind me. Then the giggling again and someone small running down the hallway and slamming a bedroom door. I threw the front door open, ready to flee.

The car was now 50 yards down the street. I was about to bolt for it anyway when I heard another stair creak behind me on the other side of the basement door. This time, it was closer, further up the stairs. Maybe only 5 steps below the main floor. I shook my head as if to shake it clear of fear. Every journalist dreams of a chance like this, of a story like this. I had to stay just long enough to get something on video.

I heard the typewriter start to click again and sprinted up the stairs, running full speed into the office. The typewriter was silent by the time I got there and I ran over to see what had been written. I sat down at the desk when I reached it, feeling suddenly tired and weak again.

jamie parsons is condemned. jamie parsons is condemned. jamie parsons is condemned.

Over and over again, all the way down the page. I took a photo with the Canon and swallowed deep breaths of air. Just then, I heard the giggling echo down the hallway again. I rose from the chair and left the office, stepping out into the darkening corridor.

The child's bedroom door was closed but I could hear scuffling and movement from behind it. I slowly opened it praying to find animals, but knowing I wouldn't.

All of the dolls in the room were still in place, only now all their heads were turned toward the door. They were looking at *me*.

I heard another giggle on my right and noticed movement out of the corner of my eye. I slammed the door shut and fell back against the banister in terror. I couldn't do this. I slowly got up, tired and shaky. I needed to leave. I ran by the sewing room door, which was open again, and this time there were only 3 mannequins left in the room.

I didn't stop to wonder where the others had gone. I bolted down the stairs as I felt and heard something else run up them, stomping loudly the entire way.

I had been wrong. So wrong. I needed to get out of here. I ran at the front door and turned the handle desperately, my stomach dropping when I found it locked. I ran down the hall, through the living room, and into the kitchen, pulling on the backdoor and screaming in frustration when it wouldn't open either.

"Where ya goin? He he he." I heard from the living room. The dolls. Jesus, the dolls. I stumbled back into the room which was now lit by a single tall, black lamp in the corner. There was a doll lying on the floor in the middle of the room that hadn't been there before.

Knowing my fate was probably already sealed, I walked over and picked her up off the floor. Her head hung limp behind her as any dolls' would.

"What did you say to me?" I breathed.

Nothing.

"What the fuck did you say to me?!" I demanded as I shook the doll, my sanity quickly slipping away.

The doll slowly picked its head up and smiled, breaking the stitching on its mouth.

"You're never leaving, Jamie. You're going to be just like me."

I screamed and threw the doll against the wall. The lamp went out then and I heard the doll run off into the darkness.

I put my head between my knees breathing hard now. I couldn't catch my breath. This house was draining me, it was sucking the life from me, just like the rest of the town. I was so tired.

I walked out into the hallway to make my way to the foyer again to try the door. The windows on the house were barred, it was my only chance. As I turned the corner in the hallway I fell back against the wall, dropping my Canon. A sheeted mannequin was standing in the middle of the hallway, 15 feet away.

Tears poured down my face as I noticed for the first time that this mannequin had legs - and feet. Another doll. It was another doll. A human sized doll.

Not knowing what else to do, I bent down and picked up my Canon and then slowly raised the shaking camera to my eye, peering through the viewfinder. I snapped the picture and when I lowered it again, I screamed. It was now right in front of me, the doll, and it mumbling something unintelligible from under the sheet.

I ran. I ran for my life, down the hall and this time, I had no reflection in the mirror. I didn't even want to think about where my reflection was right then. As I took the stairs two at a time, I heard whatever was on the basement stairs take another step up - it had to be nearly at the top.

I ran into the master bedroom and slammed the door, then sunk down to floor and beat my fists against it, screaming. I had such sever muscle weakness at this point, I could barely move. How was I ever going to escape this place? Was I going to die here from a horrible death? I raised my head to look out the window for my car. I finally saw it - in the darkness - at the end of the street. I leaned back against the door, weak and sick and I slowly slipped into unconsciousness.

When I awoke again, I realized I wasn't safe and sound back home like I'd been dreaming but laying on the bed in the nightmare house. And something was sitting on me, weighing me down. I shot up and noticed I had been tucked under the covers and the entire quilt on top of me was covered in little dolls. They were so many of them trapping me there, all looking in my direction. But the worst was at the end of the bed. There, leaning toward me over the footboard, was a mannequin. But I now knew it wasn't a mannequin - it was a doll. And it was mumbling at me angrily.

I gasped as the sheet slowly started to slip off the mannequin and I fell out of bed onto the floor. I heard the dolls giggling as I clawed my way out of the room. I didn't know where to go. With the windows barred and the doors locked the only way out seemed to be the small port window in the attic which I wasn't even sure I could fit my body through. I dragged myself to the attic door and tried the lock, hoping maybe, just maybe, the lock had switched on this door as well. It had. I slammed the door open and flew up the stairs.

I crawled up the last step into the attic and turned toward the window. My heart fell into the floor. Oh, there was the port window, sure enough, and I might just have been able to squeeze through it, too. But between it and I was a sea of doll, both small and large. They sat and stood in two rows, facing each other. There had to be hundreds of them. I screamed in terrified frustration and in perfect unison every head turned to look at me. I recoiled in horror and fell down the attic stairs, hitting the second floor with a hard thud.

The typewriter was clicking away again, but I didn't want to know what it was typing. I pushed myself up and shuffled down the stairs. There had to be another way out; I wouldn't die here, I couldn't.

When I got to the bottom of the staircase, I turned to face the fun house mirror in the foyer. It was half a second behind me again. I watched it, mesmerized, in a trace, hoping to learn its secrets. A pale, thin face that I didn't recognize stared blankly back at me. I had changed in the few hours I had been here; I looked like a corpse.

Suddenly I heard a loud knocking on the basement door behind me. The thing had reached the top of the stairs.

I spun toward the basement door and fell to my knees in my weakened state. I happened to glance under my arm as I stood up and saw that my reflection had remained standing and facing me. I turned back to the mirror but by the time I did, it was just a half second behind me again. I leaned forward toward the mirror watching it take a moment to follow. I blinked, but this time when I opened my eyes, its eyes were open as well. My reflection suddenly sneered at me and slammed the glass with its fist from the other side. The mirror cracked like a spider web and I stumbled back in terror falling through the basement door that now stood open.

I felt every jolt and bump and crack as I tumbled down the stairs and when my body finally came to rest at the bottom, it was in agony. I raised my head up just in time to see the basement door slam shut at the top of the stairs leaving me in utter darkness. And then I saw no more.

This time when I came to the room was well lit. I was lying on a concrete floor, on a dirty, beige sheet. I tried to lift myself up but my arms gave out when I saw the dozen covered mannequins standing around me. They were facing a large portrait which hung on the wall. I used strength I'd thought long depleted to stand and walk to the portrait. It was absolutely entrancing.

The portrait was of a woman but it was painted to look like a mirrored reflection of the room I was standing in, dolls and all. In the middle of the painting stood a tall, dark haired solemn woman in a maroon dress. She looked almost familiar to me. No, she *was* familiar to me. I had seen her in town as a child, I was sure of it. But that didn't make sense because the woman was dressed like a 17th century noble.

I leaned closer to study her face. The lady in the painting has less wrinkles than the woman I remember, but she had those same dark-brown, angry eyes.

The portrait blinked. I fell backwards, into a mannequin which somehow managed not to fall over. It had regained its own balance. This must be one of the ones with feet. I looked around the room. They all had feet.

As my body began to shake I turned back to the painting and watched the woman's face slowly curl into a smile.

"Stay away from me!" I screamed at it and ran for the stairs. I pushed my way through the mannequins, feeling their hands grab at my shirt, trying to pull me back.

I took the stairs three at a time and when I reached the top, I threw the door open and slammed it behind me. My reflection was still standing in the middle of the mirror, unmoving except for its eyes, which watched me with quiet ire. I couldn't get out the front door, but maybe there was one other way out.

I dragged myself into the library and grabbed the first chair I stumbled into. Running back to the foyer, I raised the chair to throw into the mirror. In the half-second pause it hung over my head, I heard feet: little pitter-patters and loud human-sized steps running down the staircase to my right and up the basement steps behind me. I could see them coming out of the corner of my eye but dared not look.

I threw the chair full force against the mirror as my reflection continued to sneer at me. It shattered and revealed a hole, a black abyss on the other side. Running on pure adrenaline, I pushed myself into it. I heard the dolls follow but I ran and ran in the dark - for hours it seemed - until I finally tripped over something and fell.

I listened for footsteps. Silence.

Looking up, I saw I was in the woods next to the house. It was dark outside and there was nothing behind me or around me. I had no idea where I'd just come from. I could see the house just behind me, it sat quiet and serene - but I knew better.

Gaining my feet, I kept running. I fell several times almost succumbing to the darkness before I pulled myself back up. I kept moving down the road, desperate to find my car. When I finally saw it on the moonlit horizon, I pulled the keys from my pocket and all but fell into the driver's seat.

Not wasting a moment, I started the car and peeled off down the street. I drove as fast as I could out of Keeling, twice slamming on the brakes when I thought I saw a sheet-covered mannequin in my rear-view mirror.

I never returned to Keeling, or Missouri for that matter. At least, not physically... Even though my *body* escaped, I never actually did. I'm still there. Every time I dream - or even close my eyes - I am back there, running from room to room. The dolls find new ways to surprise and terrify me every night. If I daydream, it is the same. I am only a hollowed shell of who I was. My consciousness and my body are here but my soul is trapped in Keeling.

In case you're wondering, I escaped with my Canon around my neck but the pictures were all empty, as black as the hole that was Keeling on the satellite images.

Sometimes even after I wake up in the night, I see a mannequin in the corner of my room. I know I'm in California, but I'm also in Keeling, in that house, at the same time. I have been condemned to it and a part of me lives there. Whatever the house's fate, it is my fate as well.

Every night in my dreams the dolls try to pull me back into that basement. So far, I have resisted, but I can't hide forever. Someday, they will drag me back into the black abyss. And what awaits me there, I do not know.

COPPER CANYON

SATURDAY

07-23-2011
Transcript of call from witness R.L.
1:20 p.m.

Dispatcher: *911, what's your emergency?*

Caller R.L.: *I need to report an accident. Somebody- a car just went over the barrier on the I-17. Northbound.*

Dispatcher: *Sir, do you see a mile marker?*

Caller R.L.: *Yeah, we're, ah, we're outside of Camp Verde in Copper Canyon. I'm walking towards the mile marker. There's- it looks like 282.*

Dispatcher: *How many vehicles are involved?*

Caller R.L.: *I think it's- oh fuck, did you hear that? Whatever ran off the cliff just exploded. There's smoke coming up over the side of the mountain.*

Dispatcher: *We've got someone on the way.*

07-23-2011
Transcript of call from witness D.W.
1:22 p.m.

Dispatcher: *Yavapai County 911, what's the emergency?*

Caller D.W.: *Yeah, an SUV just went over the cliff. The car is on fire and there are people screaming. It's...it's fucking chaos out here.*

Dispatcher: *Is this Northbound 17 just south of...Camp Verde?*

Caller D.W.: *Yes. People are trying to get down the cliff.*

Dispatcher: *Can you see any injuries, ma'am?*

Caller D.W.: *Yes, there's people, there's* [inaudible] *in the ravine outside the car. There's, oh my god, there's kids. There's kids and an adult. A woman, I think.*

Dispatcher: *Is anyone injured?*

Caller D.W.: *No, they're all dead.*

FRIDAY

I leaned back against my truck and took a few deep drags of my cigarette before snubbing it out on the tire and flicking it under the car next to me. Stella should be pulling up with the kids any minute and she'd flip her shit if she saw me smoking.

As I watched for headlights coming around the corner of the hotel parking lot I popped a breath mint and took a swig of water. Phoenix was hot in July - oppressively hot. And even though the sun was almost down I knew I couldn't last out here much longer.

While it was a nice escape from my frigid hometown of Flagstaff in the winter, Phoenix left much to be desired in the summertime. I tried to come down as infrequently as possible during the during the summer months but sometimes work made that impossible. I always hated leaving the mountains. Even though the valley was only two and a half hours away from Flag, it may as well have been a thousand miles. My small, mountain town and the sprawling, desert city might as well be different countries all together.

I saw the headlights of Stella's silver Mazda peek around the corner of the building and I pushed myself off the truck.

She pulled into a nearby space and I smiled as I went to greet her. I could tell by the look on her face when she got out that she was worn down.

"How was the drive?" I asked her as I opened the back door to let Aiden and Wyatt out.

"Long. You know I hate that drive, I don't know how you do it so often."

I laughed. "Well that's what I get paid for. A necessary evil to keep my family living in luxury."

"Dad, do I have to go tonight?" Aiden yelled from the trunk of the car where he was trying, in vain, to pull his overnight bag out of the jostled mess of luggage.

"What you don't like dressing up?"

He made a face at me. "I hate it. Plus there's not gonna be other kids there."

"That's not true; Dani and Paul's kids will be there."

"They're girls, they don't count."

"You'll have your brother."

"Daaaaad, he's only three."

"Aiden!" Stella yelled as she propped the door into the hotel open. "Quit complaining and get your brother inside. What's the room number, Matt?"

"323. Door's open."

Aiden took his brother's hand and walked him inside and down the hall. When Stella and I were alone, I eyed the trunk with confusion.

"Why so many bags? You know we're only here for tonight, right?"

"Yes, Matt, I know that." Stella rubbed her temples.

"You feeling okay?"

"Yeah, I'm fine. Just tired."

"This heat probably isn't helping either. Do you want to go inside? I'll get the bags."

"No, I'll help. Have you seen Dani and Paul yet this week?"

"Not yet. They've been busy."

Dani and Paul were very close friends of my wife and I. The only reason Stella and kids were even in Phoenix was to attend their tenth anniversary dinner this evening. I'd been here all week working on campus.

As much as I loved our friends I couldn't wait to depart in the morning for higher elevations and cooler temperatures – even with Dani and Paul's three daughters in tow. Stella had graciously offered to watch their kids while they spent the next week in Mexico.

"Do you have an Excedrin, hon?"

"Inside. Is your head hurting again?" I asked.

"Just a bit."

"You've been tired and nauseous a lot in the past few days, Stel. Are you sure you're okay?"

"Yeah. I've just been getting a lot of headaches lately."

SATURDAY

07-23-2011
Eyewitness account of K.B.
10:23 a.m.

I don't know why I noticed it, maybe just because it was sitting there for so long. It was a blue suburban - 2009 or 2010 model maybe? – and it was parked on the side of the highway outside of New River just idling. I had to take multiple trips in and out of New River that morning for work and that truck probably sat there for 25 minutes. It barely fit on the shoulder even though it was parked right up next to the guard rail. It was definitely a road hazard. I was planning to check on the car the next time I went out but by the time I got back it was gone.

07-23-2011
Eyewitness account of L.L.
11:01 a.m.

I was in the far right lane getting off of Northbound 17 at Exit 144 in Black Canyon City. This blue suburban suddenly merges over two lanes and cuts me off. It was so sudden that I was surprised it didn't roll. I got pretty angry and laid on my horn. I was going to pull up next to the truck at the stop sign but I saw little kids in the car so I just kept driving. The woman in the driver's seat didn't even look at me. She looked so dazed - I'm not even sure she heard my horn.

FRIDAY

"You look amazing, Stel."

My wife, after 8 years of marriage, was still one of the most beautiful women I'd ever seen. Not that she believed it, of course; in fact I was pretty sure she never had.

Stella was a few years older me and I knew that had always bothered her. When I first met my wife she was a quiet, nervous girl who still lived at home with her parents. We met at an engagement party for a mutual friend and I used the next few months to slowly nudge her out of her shell. It didn't take me long to realize that Stella was already in love with me by the time I'd formally met her. I married my wife a year later and got her pregnant immediately. Stella was over the moon, all she'd ever wanted was to be a mother. She told me the day of Aiden's birth was the happiest day of her life.

Maybe that's what she needs, I mused as I watched my wife lather her arms with hotel supplied vanilla scented lotion. *Maybe another baby would make her happy again.*

Stella had fallen into a sort of depression in the last year and refused to go to the doctor. I did the best I could to make the good times great and the bad times more tolerable for her.

"Did you hear me, babe? You look stunning."

"I'm glad you still think that," she said without looking at me.

"You know I've always thought that."

Stella finally looked away from the mirror and gave me an impish smirk. "Would be nice if you showed me....physically, more often." She winked.

I sighed and walked over to wrap my arms around her lotion-slick shoulders. God knows, we hadn't been intimate in months. And I knew that a sensitive girl like Stella must be going crazy, thinking I was falling out of love with her or some other nonsense.

"Well, if we didn't have five kids in the house over the weekend..." I trailed off and gave her my most seductive smile in the mirror.

She frowned. "You just always seem to have an excuse, Matt. If you're not working late on campus, you're down in Phoenix. I just don't understand why you get pulled down to that campus so much when you teach at the Flagstaff campus."

I dropped my arms from her shoulders and ran a hand through my messy hair. "Stel, I've told you, I'm helping out the chemistry department down there. I have to continue to do that if I want tenure."

Stella walked away from me with a dismissive wave.

"Boys!" She yelled, knocking on the door to our adjoining room with the kids. "Aiden! Is Wyatt dressed? Bring him in here; we're leaving for dinner in a few."

SATURDAY

07-23-2011
Eyewitness account of Officer J. Pendlo (Badge #2881)
11:27 a.m.

I had a driver pulled over in Black Canyon City on Squaw Valley Road in the shoulder of the Westbound lane. As I was running his driver's license I noticed a dark blue 2009 Chevy Suburban stopped on the dirt road off Maggie Mine Road leading to the abandoned dog track. Plate number 22D4N12. The back bumper was heavily dented and the passenger side of the vehicle was sideswiped.

A woman had the back door open and was leaning against the vehicle's frame talking to someone in the backseat. I heard yelling coming from inside the vehicle. The woman stumbled back a bit and then climbed into the backseat of the suburban. She appeared to be distressed. I intended to go investigate the vehicle when I finished writing the traffic violation. The vehicle was gone by the time I pulled out some minutes later. I searched the area but I believe the vehicle was back on the highway by then.

07-23-2011
Eyewitness account of E.S.
11:27 a.m.

I was pulled over for running a stop sign and I was texting my wife while the officer was back running my plates. I looked up and saw a woman and a maybe 9 year old girl standing outside the car. The woman was trying to walk forward and the girl was pushing her back trying to get her to sit down. At one point the girl got back into the car and the woman slid down the car to the ground. She looked really out of it. Then all of the sudden she got a sort of second wind and sprung up and walked around the other side of the car, jerked the door open and started yelling at the girl inside. I could hear a couple kids in there crying. She had her hand in the car trying to reach someone. Then she crawled into the backseat and about a minute later the car left.

FRIDAY

I shook Paul's hand as I grabbed a scotch off the bar. "Congrats, old man! Ten years is quite an accomplishment in this day and age."

"Well, you're right behind me, there Matt." He laughed.

"Very true," I said, glancing over at our wives who were talking in the corner. "But loving a woman that long is so easy when she's so beautiful." I saw her laugh then and admired the boisterous rise and fall of her chest, the swell of her breasts emerging slightly from the low cut glittering neckline of her gown. Even though she was so torn right now I hoped she knew how much I loved her.

"Thick as thieves, those two," Paul chuckling, watching the scene beside me. "Ever since college."

"Worse than sisters." I nodded as Dani picked up her youngest, Ava, and handed the squealing 1 year old to my wife. Stella laughed louder than I had heard in the past year and bounced little Ava on her hip. I smiled as I watched her. Another baby may be the solution after all.

"Uncle Matt?" My attention turned to the lovely young lady standing behind me, Paul's oldest. Izzy was intelligent like her mother but the spitting image of her father. The two had always been close. Paul put his arm around his daughter and kissed her on the head.

"Hi Izzy," I smiled, "are you excited to spend the weekend in Flagstaff? I think Aunt Stella is going to take you hiking tomorrow."

"Yeah, I'm excited. Um, Wyatt keeps trying to pull people's wine glasses off the table and he's already spilled sprite on himself."

"Ugh, that boy. Thanks for the heads up, Iz, I'll go get that little outlaw."

I found my son sitting in between Paul and Dani's other daughter, Emma, and his big brother.

"We were just holding him here. He's trying to drink the wine." Emma said confidently as Aiden nodded.

"Is that so?"

"Well, he was trying to grab it. I think he was going to drink it."

"Yeah, he was. He was, Dad, but I stopped him."

I shook my head lightheartedly and looked around for Stella. She was now sitting at a table chatting and laughing with Paul's sister, not a care in the world. I watched her for a moment and frowned. My wife wasn't one to neglect the whereabouts of her children, especially our youngest. Most of her days were spent following Wyatt around the world making sure he was safe and happy. It was very unlike her.

I picked Wyatt up from the bench. "Okay boys, it's time to start calming down. We have an early morning so I think we'll head out in about 20 minutes."

"I want to stay and play with Emma." Aiden stood up and crossed his arms.

"I thought you didn't like girls," I teased.

"Dad, STOP!" Aiden yelled so loud that people on the other side of the room turned to look. He ran out into the hall, his face reddening with every step. Emma and I both laughed and I looked over again at Stella hoping she was laughing too. But she wasn't.

Stella was sitting down at the suddenly empty table with her head in her hands, rubbing her temples.

SATURDAY

07-23-2011
Transcript of call from witness C.M.
12:08 p.m.

DPS Operator: *Highway Patrol, where can I direct your call?*

Caller C.K.: *Hi, yeah, sorry, I didn't know who to call but I thought 911 probably wasn't it. Ah, there's a truck in-*

DPS Operator: *Do you have a road safety issue, ma'am?*

Caller C.K.: *Yeah, I'm about 5 miles north of Cordes Lakes on the I-17 and there's a truck in the left lane going slow. Like, really slow.*

DPS Operator: *I'm sorry ma'am, but we don't handle those types of calls. Would you like me to put you through to emergency services?*

Caller C.K.: *No, I don't think it's an emergency. But I passed her and she's going about 25 miles per hour in a 65 mile per hour zone. She just has this, like, blank look on her face. She needs to get off the road, because she keeps crossing the middle line. She looks really out of it.*

DPS Operator: *Would you like me to put you through to emergency services?*

Caller C.K.: *No, it's fine. I'm way past her now, I just thought someone should know about it but yeah, I guess, I don't- I don't need to report it at this point.*

07-23-2011
Transcript of voicemail from the cell phone of Paul Grigg (602-307-29xx)
12:14 p.m.

"Daddy, I'm scared, can you come get me- me? Aunt Stella doesn't feel [inaudible] *she's acting really weird and scary. I don't understand what she's saying when she talks and Wyatt won't* [pause] *stop crying and we're scared. Ava fell asleep. She won't listen to me, Dad, I told her to call you but she wouldn't so the last time she* [inaudible] [pause] *I took her phone. Please come get us or send Uncle Matt to come get us. I don't know what to do and I'm really scared.* [crying] *Aunt Stella keeps hitting stuff with the car and I saw her throw up* [crying] [inaudible] *driving right. Please call me back, Daddy, or text the phone so she doesn't hear you."*

FRIDAY

"We'll swing by around 8 tomorrow and grab the girls. What time is your flight?"

"10:30 but the earlier you get to our house the better. Dani and I wouldn't mind some alone time." Paul leaned back on his heels and winked at his wife.

"Alright, alright, Matt and I know how it goes," Stella giggled and leaned her head against my shoulder. "How does 7:30 sound?"

"Earlier." Paul growled wrapping his arms around Dani's waist and nuzzling her ear.

I'd known my wife so well and for so long that I detected the instant she felt uncomfortable and intimidated. She laughed nervously and I could feel the envy radiating off of her. Stella had always wanted the sort of open affection, no apologies relationship that Dani and Paul shared. It had just never been that way with us. I opened my mouth to break the tension but Stella spoke first.

"You guys are like kids. Having sex all the time and in Mexico no less. Maybe you'll babysit for us some weekend and we can go to Mexico."

"Stel, are you drunk?" Paul teased. "You're terrified of Mexico!"

"You know I don't drink! And I'd risk being kidnapped in Mexico…Matt would protect me." Stella smiled up at me with the sort of eyes I hadn't seen in so long I'd forgotten how beautiful they were.

I wrapped my arm around her and pulled her to me.

"Girls! In the car!" Paul yelled to his daughters who were running around the empty parking lot. "I swear they're usually not this crazy." Paul shook his head.

"Oh don't worry about it;" Stella laughed, "we've got lots of room to run on our property. They're in safe hands."

SATURDAY

07-23-2011
Eyewitness account of J.S.
12:37 p.m.

    I was buying cigarettes at the Chevron in Cordes Lakes when I heard somebody slam on their breaks outside and punch the horn. I looked out the window and saw a blue SUV drive by, just as calm as can be while this guy in a white pickup is yelling out his window at it.

    Then I was driving over to Wagners and I saw the same blue SUV going down Stagecoach Trail. The driver pulled over to park the car on the shoulder and then suddenly changed her mind or something and flipped a u-turn instead. The tires left tracks in the road. I could see some little kids' heads bobbing around through the back windshield. I decided to follow her because I thought maybe she was drunk. We see a lot of drunk drivers around here.

    So I get in my car and follow her back down Stagecoach. She starts speeding up as she gets closer to the highway. I estimate she got up to about 75 and the limit on Stagecoach is 40. I lost her when she ran the light at Oasis. I would have called 911 to report her but I didn't have my phone.

07-23-2011
Transcript of call from witness M.M.
12:52 p.m.

Dispatcher: *911, what's your emergency?*

Caller C.M.: *Hi, I'm calling to report a truck going the wrong way down the 69.*

Dispatcher: *You said the vehicle is going the wrong way?*

Caller C.M.: *Yeah, he's going north, or...south, sorry, in the Northbound lane. Outside of Spring Valley.*

Dispatcher: *He's going south in the Northbound lane?*

Caller C.M.: *Yes.*

Dispatcher: *Can you describe the vehicle, sir?*

Caller C.M..: *It's like a blue colored SUV. A Tahoe, I think.*

Dispatcher: *Can you tell me-"*

Caller C.M.: *Oh shit! It just hit the guard rail. And it's-* [laughing] *it's still going!*

07-23-2011
Transcript of call from witness F.D.
1:11 p.m.

Dispatcher: *911*

Caller F.D.: *Hi, I need to report a speeding truck on the I-17.*

Dispatcher: *You said it's speeding?*

Caller FD: *Yeah, it's speeding. It's going at least 100 miles an hour.*

Dispatcher: *Where are you on the interstate?*

Caller FD: *I just passed the exit for the 169. He's about a half mile ahead of me.*

Dispatcher: *Is the vehicle in the Southbound or Northbound lane, sir?*

Caller FD: *Northbound. It's headed into Copper Canyon.*

SATURDAY

"Stella. Stella, wake up, we have to get the boys ready."
She didn't move a muscle.
"Baby, are you okay?"
"Yeah," she moaned, "Just another migraine."

"Stel, we gotta get you to the doctor. These chronic headaches worry me." "No, I'm fine, really, I'm fine. I already saw my doctor about it and he said it's likely the start of menopause."

I tried not to show the surprise on my face. I must have failed.

"Yes, Matthew, I'm going through menopause because I'm older than you." She snapped. "You knew that when you married me."

"It's not that, I just-"

"Save it." Stella rolled away from me and buried her face in the pillows. "Just go."

"Go?"

"Yeah, just start heading home. I'll be right behind you. I just need to sleep for another half an hour."

"I can't. We told Paul and Dani we would pick the girls up early."

"Fuck them. And fuck you for caring so much about their sex life."

I got up from the bed and awkwardly straightened my tie in the mirror just to give myself something to do. It seemed I had been right about Stella's feelings of inadequacy last night.

I'd made a move on her as soon as we'd gotten the kids to bed the night before. I'd pulled her into me and slid my hands down her hips, then slowly pulled her shirt up over her head. I'd let my hand slip down into her lacy bra. I'd kissed her neck...

She'd jerked away from me then, complaining that she suddenly felt nauseous. I believed her too. Her face had grown pale and her hands were shaking slightly as she unzipped her pants and threw them in the corner.

Then she'd gone straight to sleep.

"I really don't give a shit about their sex life, Stella, I care about being where we said we'd be when we said we'd be there."

"I'm sorry," she whimpered from the bed after a moment. "It just hurts so much."

"Why don't I take the boys and go get the girls and then I'll come back here. It'll give you some time to sleep."

"No, it's, it's fine. I'll take an Excedrin and I'll go get the girls. You go ahead and head north, somebody needs to let the dogs out this morning."

"Okay, sweetie. Want me to take the boys?"

"No, let them sleep in. Just take my car and leave me the suburban."

"Are you sure?"

"I'm sure. I'll take the kids."

SATURDAY

07-23-2011
Transcript from interview of Danielle E. Grigg

"Stella showed up just after 8 o'clock. She seemed [pause] *normal. She came to the door, she was smiling, and she picked up Ava and tickled her. I mean she was just normal, old Stella. I didn't know, I couldn't tell that anything was wrong,* [pause] *um,* [pause] *excuse I'm, I'm sorry.* [pause] [crying] *I couldn't tell that anything was wrong with her. Paul came to the door with all the kids' bags and gave her a hug. She hugged him back.*

He walked all the luggage out to Matt's car and I kissed and hugged my girls goodbye. [pause] *I'm sorry. Um, I kissed my girls goodbye and I held Ava for a minute. And then Paul kissed the kids goodbye. He talked to Izzy for a while because she was crying and didn't want to leave. Those two, they were like best friends.*

Then we put the kids in the car and Paul and I said hi to the boys. Izzy, Ava and Wyatt were in the middle row and Emma and Aiden were in the back. Then she — Stella, sorry - hugged us both and told us to have a safe flight. She seemed happy, she told the kids they were going to have a Disney sing-along. [crying] *Then she backed out of the driveway with my children and I never saw them again."*

7-23-2011
Transcript of call from witness I.N.
1:16 p.m.

Dispatcher: *Yavapai County 911.*

Caller I.N.: *Um, oh god. Fuck. Oh Christ, there's, this, ah, there's a car that was in front of me and it just went over the guard rail into the canyon. Just, oh god, he just* [inaudible] *and went over. He didn't even slow down at all. I'm still going, should I turn around?*

Dispatcher: *Where are you, sir?*

Caller I.N.: *On the 17. In the canyon.*

07-23-2011
Eyewitness account of T.N.
1:16 p.m.

As soon as I saw the car go over, I stopped on the West shoulder of the road. I'd noticed that truck earlier because it'd been weaving in and out of traffic as it approached me. Something was definitely happening with the driver. She was really calm and steady, like real oddly serene, almost oblivious to what was going on outside of the car. She cut in front of me but I was prepared for it so I slowed down without a problem. She didn't. She just kept going in that trajectory right over the side of the mountain.

Other people started pulling over too and we tried to get down the cliff but it's a pretty sheer drop right there. Then about, well, when I guess we were about halfway down, the truck caught on fire. There were bodies all over the place. Little kids, mostly. I've never seen anything like it. I saw photos of the accident on the news but they were taken after the police had been there and cleaned up a bit. When we first got down into the canyon, it was like looking into hell. All the bodies were still burning. Everyone was dead.

SATURDAY

I made my first call to Stella's cell phone at 11:04. It rang for a while and then went to voicemail. This didn't worry me as my wife usually turned her cell phone on silent when she was driving through the mountains; that road had always made her nervous.

At 11:30 I called again, and this time someone sent it to voicemail. I still didn't worry too much. I'd talked to Dani before her flight left that morning and she'd told me Stella hadn't come by to pick up the girls until 8:15 and that she'd planned to get the kids some breakfast before she got on the road. A 2 hour drive would put her in close to 11 but my wife was a slow and careful driver.

At noon I started to pace around my office trying Stella's cell phone off and on.

By 1 p.m. I was a wreck.

At 1:14 I got a frantic call from Paul about a voicemail he'd received from Izzy. I immediately called the police and reported my wife missing and the phone call from inside the car. A woman called me back after the longest 40 minutes of my life. She told me there had been an accident and that they were sending someone to my house.

Everything that made me human had suddenly been stripped away from me. I lost everything that day.

Paul and Dani flew back from Cancun that night and got the news right when they landed. Paul had to be sedated at the airport. Dani was just numb.

Someone brought me what was left of our personal effects from the crash: Emma's suitcase and Stella's overnight bag. All the others had been destroyed in the accident.

Stella's body was too badly burned to do any conclusive toxicology on her. No one had any idea what had happened to my wife, why she'd been behaving so strangely or how she lost control of the car. The investigation went on until December of 2012 when the case was closed by DPS. No one knew what happened to Stella but the general consensus, all evidence accounting, was that some sort of medical event had occurred on the day of the crash: possibly a stroke or a series of strokes.

I fought hard to clear Stella's name in the press; they painted her as a drunk and a pill popper. The media also compared her case to something that had happened in New York a few years earlier, the Schuler case. But Stella didn't drink - ever - or take pills recreationally and she loved her children more than the air she breathed. I hired a private investigator and a lawyer to help me get her body exhumed and retested. Afterward I was told the results were similar to the first tests but that this time the ME had ruled her secondary cause of death "Vehicle Crash due to an Unknown Medical Event".

The press finally back off.

Paul killed himself just before Christmas the same year of the accident. Dani told me he locked himself in his office every day and listened to Izzy's voicemail over and over until one day he hung himself from a cross beam in his daughter's room.

Dani and I bonded deeply in our grief. We had both lost so much, almost everything. We talked and cried and suffered together for years. And all along Stella's suitcase sat in my closet. I could never bring myself to unpack it - to unpack her - from my life. But then Dani moved in with me and my soul began to mend. And for the first time since the accident, I could see ahead of the agonizing pain to a more tolerable existence. I was finally ready to let it all go, to let her go. To emerge from under the crippling darkness into a dull, muted light that I knew would grow brighter with time.

And so one day, I opened the suitcase. And found out what really happened to Stella that day.

On top of my wife's neatly folded clothes was a note she had written to me in black marker. It was only six words, six short words that cast me back into hell, never to return. *I know about you and Dani.*

It was written on a liquor store receipt.

Walker

CHRISTMAS MAGIC

Mom says you have to believe in Santa if you want presents on Christmas.

Sometimes I find this hard to do, like when I see Santa at the mall and he looks different from the Santa I saw last year. If I mention this to my mom she tells me never to talk about that. She says if I do, I won't get any presents on Christmas. She told me to always assume that it's just Santa's Christmas magic at work.

Last Christmas I took my little sister to the park. I had snow ball fights with my friends while she built a snow man.

We saw Santa at the park that day. He came over and handed each of us little, wrapped presents. He told us that we were all good boys and girls. He told my sister that her present was in his sleigh because it was too big to carry. He asked her to help him.

My sister went with him, but she never came back. The police officers asked us so many questions but we all insisted it was just Santa - big, jolly and red. That was all we knew.

People were sad that my sister went with Santa so I got lots of presents that year. I'm so glad I didn't tell anyone that Santa had looked a lot like our neighbor, Mr. Wilkens. And I'm glad I didn't tell them that I saw my sister get into his blue pick-up truck instead of a sleigh. Mom says never to talk about that stuff, that it's just Santa's Christmas magic at work. And she says you have to believe in Santa's magic if you want presents on Christmas.

IT COMES ON CHRISTMAS

I never thought I'd be here again: sitting in a foreign police station with tear stains on my cheeks and a cup of cold coffee in my hands. I feel numb. I feel dead.

Dan has been separated from me for questioning, just as he was 7 years before, though this time the detectives speak English instead of Portuguese.

All we'd wanted was to take Amelia on a quiet Christmas holiday out of the country, and away from the public eye. She was having a very difficult time adjusting to her first year of primary school. And even though she was only five, the press would find her now and again and ask her horrible questions that always left her in tears.

Amelia has learned over the years that she lives in a large, empty shadow.

Seven years ago, while we were on holiday in Brazil, Amelia's older sister disappeared on Christmas Eve. Linny had been six at the time and Amelia not yet born.

Linny was never found.

I remember, all those years ago, walking back to the hotel from the lounge to check on Linny. I remember opening the door to the sound of the TV blaring Nightline in the small sitting area. I remember stumbling down the hallway, bubbly and a bit drunk, eager to get back to the party.

I remember opening Linny's door. I remember being confused. I remember yelling her name over and over. And I remember Dan, pulling me up off the floor some minutes later.

That night begat a long, fruitless and very high profile search for our daughter. The investigation was a circus: the police focused on all the wrong people, evidence was overlooked or mishandled, and Dan and I were judged guilty in the court of public opinion. Everyone thought we knew more than we said.

But we didn't.

We are, admittedly, very wealthy people. Our children have always been spoiled rotten. We spared no luxuries for ourselves. The public loved to hate us. And every intimacy of our lives was torn wide open for all to see.

It took less than a month for our affairs to come out in the press. Publicly Dan and I declared we had a mutually agreed upon open marriage. But privately we grew to hate each other. The lies and the secrets overwhelmed us.

It was only when we had Amelia two years later that we fell back in love. Our names were finally cleared as suspects when she turned three, though suspicion remained. Linny's case disappeared into the empty darkness of the cold world, just as Linny herself had. Old wounds were beginning to heal. Our lives were becoming livable again. My husband and I loved each other. Amelia had a future.

Until tonight.

I'd only gone down to the bar for a moment, just enough time to hand Dan his wallet and have a quick chat with new friends. I wanted to return to out room quickly. Dan and I were understandably overcautious about leaving Amelia but I also needed to fill her stocking and place her presents under out makeshift Christmas tree.

She had looked so peaceful, sleeping there on our bed. I hadn't wanted to wake her. I locked the door behind me, telling myself that I would be quick.

The feeling began gnawing at me in the elevator on the way back up to our floor. I pushed it away as unfounded paranoia. But when the elevator dinged and the doors opened on our floor, I knew: something was terribly wrong.

I ran down the hallway to our room where the door remained locked. I slid my keycard through the reader and threw the door open violently.

Amelia wasn't on the bed. I called her name and looked for her everywhere as tears poured down my cheeks.

And then I screamed. I screamed and screamed until hotel security was called.

It was several hours before I came out of my shock. I was sitting in the police station, they were asking me questions. They told me Dan was down the hall and that everyone in the hotel with access to our room was being questioned. But my little girl is gone. She's gone forever, just like Linny. And now I realize there is no hope. Now I know the police will never find her, just like her sister.

I can finally admit it now, to myself; I have no choice: the night Linny disappeared I did see something. I remember that I didn't tell anyone because I'd been drunk at the time and it was such an impossible thing.

But then I saw it again tonight. And now I know what happened to my daughter all those years ago.

You see, I remember walking into the Linny's room. I remember seeing the empty bed. I remember calling her name. And I remember the dark figure that was standing in the corner of her room.

And it wasn't a human being.

The creature was impossibly tall with a long face, pale yellow eyes, and the hooves and antlers of a goat. He held an unconscious Linny under his arm and muffled screaming was coming from a large burlap sack he carried on his back.

I remember dropping to my knees. I yelled at the thing that my daughter wasn't naughty, she was spoiled - it was my fault, take me instead. But the creature just hissed at me, and seemed to laugh, and by the time Dan found me the thing was gone.

But I hadn't believed any of this had really happened. I'd thought of myself as a sad, hallucinating drunk until tonight. But then this evening, I saw him again. Not in the corner of the room or in the shadows, no, I'd seen him clear as day - in the mirror. Amelia's body was tucked under his arm and the small hands of children were reaching out from the familiar burlap sack on his back.

They were still screaming.

ROOM 733

The Suicide Room. That's what they called room 733 - as if I didn't have enough to worry about on my first day as a freshman.

We had assigned to dorm room 734 which, it turns out, wasn't one of the nice add-on rooms in the south hall. No, we found ourselves in the older wing of the building on the 7th floor. I wasn't too bummed out, though; at least they'd honored my request to room with my best friend.

Lydia and I spent most of the morning moving ourselves in. By the time our Resident Advisor came by I was taping up posters and Lydia was reading.

"Hi girls, I'm Beth!" chirped the bubbly blonde girl as she bounded into our room. "I'll be your RA this year."

"Hi," I nodded at her.

"Wow, you girls really work fast," she said taking in our made beds and hung up clothes.

Beth picked up a drawing of Cthulhu that Lydia had done over the summer. She turned it sideways, studying it.

"Is this the kraken from Pirates of the Caribbean?"

Lydia glared at her over the top of her book.

"So anyway," the RA continued, "I know our hall isn't as new as the south hall but trust me, there's a lot of history here. This building is almost 60 years old."

"Yes, I can see that." I said looking around. "The rooms are pretty small."

"Well, people were smaller in the 50s." Beth shrugged.

"Really." Lydia said flatly.

"Yep, really." Beth pursed her lips and just continued to stand there, while the room filled with awkward silence.

"So," I said, "the corner room next to us - 733, is it? It looks a lot bigger than our room. Is anyone assigned to that room or could we maybe-"

"Oh, you don't want that room." Beth interrupted. "There were a couple suicides in there. A hanging and a jumper if I remember right. They're not assigning anyone to that room. Anyway, I'd just like to remind you that this is an all-girls floor and guys are not allowed up here after 11."

Before we could reply to her Beth clapped her hands and with a quick "well, nice meeting you" she skipped out of the room.

Lydia dropped her book on the bed and stared out into the hall. "I hate her."

"Did you hear that bomb she fucking dropped?"

"I'm going to call her Dumbshit Beth."

"Lydia, seriously. Suicides?"

"Oh, Becca, relax. Every college campus has a few suicides."

"Yeah, but in the same room?"

Lydia sighed. "Really, who cares? It's not *our* room."

"Yeah, I guess." I turned to study the little window in our room. "Can you imagine climbing out of that tiny window and jumping? You'd be alive for at least five seconds before you hit the ground."

"Oh, fuck, Becca, can you not?" Lydia glanced at the window and visibly shuddered. "You know I fucking hate heights and just talking about that shit is raising my blood pressure."

"We could always move into the suicide room," I teased her, "That one has a window on each wall."

"Fuck you."

"Okay, okay. But seriously, think about it. It would take a lot of commitment to squeeze out of that tiny window."

"Yeah, well, remember, people were apparently smaller back then." Lydia mumbled as she pushed her bed further away from the window.

*

Since Lydia was an outgoing and friendly person, we made friends at lightning speed. There were a lot of parties in those first few weeks, at one of which Lydia inevitably met a guy. I'd known the girl since we were in diapers so I fully anticipated her having a boyfriend by the end of September. His name was Mike and he wasn't anything special; just your standard frat pledge douche canoe.

After about a month on campus the novelty of college started wearing off. Lydia and I found our stride and we spent more weekends studying than drinking. Midterms were coming up in a couple weeks and I was determined to maintain a 4.0 GPA throughout my freshman year.

One night in early October I was woken up by a loud, grinding sound. I sat up in bed and strained to hear it again. Lydia was also wide awake and listening.

SLAM

What the fuck? She mouthed to me.

It wasn't unusual for there to be noise in the hallways since other people came in at all hours of the night. But this sound had definitely come from next door - the corner room.

GRIND

"Is that-"

"Yeah," Lydia whispered. "That's the window next door."

At Lydia's insistence, we kept our window closed at all times. However, there was no mistaking the sound of the window in room 733 being opened and closed again at regular intervals.

SLAM

"Who's in there?"

Lydia shrugged.

"Is someone fucking with us? Is this like initiation?"

Lydia raised her eyebrow at me. "Initiation to what?"

"I don't know. College? Maybe they're hazing the freshman?"

GRIND (it opened)

"Who is hazing freshman?"

I shrugged.

SLAM (it shut)

"Becca, I love you, but that was fucking stupid."

I threw a pillow at her. "Well, whoever it is, go tell them to knock it the fuck off."

"Me?! I'm not risking being thrown out a window."

GRIND

"Well, I'm not doing it!"

"I'm an art major. You're a political science major. YOU go lay down the law."

"Fuck that."

"Then call Dumbshit Beth. Isn't this the kind of nonsense she should deal with?"

SLAM

"I'm not calling her. Don't you put that evil on me."

"Fine," Lydia whispered loudly, "then we'll just have to ignore it."

"I have class at 7:30!" I whispered.

GRIND

"Then do something!"

"Ugh!" I got out of bed and stomped to the door, threw it open dramatically and went down the hall to pound on the door to room 733 which simply said 'Supply Room'.

"People are trying to sleep, please fucking stop." I said when there was no answer.

SLAM

"Dude, seriously..." I sighed.

I stepped back from the door and immediately noticed problem. Room 733 was padlocked shut from the outside. I hurried back to my room.

"What happened?" Lydia asked.

"I'm not going anywhere near that fucking room, again. It's locked from the outside; I don't know how anybody could get in there."

"So, you're saying it's a spooky ghost?" She laughed.

"No, I'm saying there is creepy shit going on inside a room colloquially called 'the Suicide Room'."

Lydia scoffed and rolled over to go back to sleep. "You should have been a drama major."

We didn't hear the window next door again that night but the next morning you could clearly see from outside that both windows in the corner room were now wide open.

＊

I watched the windows on room 733 for an entire week but they remained open. Occasionally at night I thought I could hear a noise next door liked marbles dropping and rolling across the floor. Since it never woke Lydia up, I didn't bother to say anything.

One afternoon I was alone in the dorm editing notes on my laptop. I had my headphones in but the music wasn't loud enough to cover the noise of someone knocking on the door.

"Come in," I said without looking up from the screen.

A moment went by and then heard I heard the knocking again. I jerked my earbuds out and slammed the laptop closed.

I turned around, "Come-"

What the fuck? The door to the hallway was wide open. I'd left it open on purpose since Ian (a junior I was dating) was supposed to be stopping by. I heard the knocking again from behind me and literally jumped out of my chair.

It had come from the other side of the room – the closet door. It was the closet that shared a wall with room 733.

"Lydia, you're not fucking funny."

Nothing.

"Lydia, I swear to god, I will punch you in your face."

Silence. I walked over to the closet door and grasped the handle.

"Lydia, you're a fucking-"

"A fucking what?"

Her voice came from the doorway – behind me. I let go of the doorknob and stumbled back, wide-eyed. Lydia threw her stuff on the bed and turned to me, crossing her arms.

"I'm a fucking what?"

"I...thought you were hiding in the closet." I said, lamely.

"What? Why?"

"Because someone was knocking on the door."

"Jesus, Becca." Lydia rubbed her forehead and walked over to the closet, throwing open the door. There was nothing there but clothes and boxes. She made a swipe of her arm as if to say: 'what now?'

"I swear-"

"Becca, there's no one here."

"I know what I heard."

We glared at each other until our little standoff was interrupted by the timely arrival of Ian.

He immediately sensed the tension in the room. "Hi, ladies... What's new?"

I gave my roommate a hostile look. "There's strange shit is going on in that room next door. But that's not new."

'Which room? 735? Or the empty one?"

"The *empty* one." Lydia emphasized.

"733. Yeah, I'm not surprised. That's the suicide room."

"Right, we heard about the deaths." I sat down on my bed.

"Yeah, it's pretty fucked up. Three suicides all in one dorm room."

"Three?" Lydia raised her eyebrow. "We were told there were two."

"Well there were a couple people in the 70s and then some guy about ten years ago. He jumped out the window."

Lydia and I both shuddered. Although she was much worse, we were both terrified of heights. A falling death was about the worst thing I could think of.

"I will admit that three suicides in the same dorm room is fucking disturbing." Lydia said in an apologetic tone.

"Yeah, I heard there's something in that room." Ian said.

"Like what?"

"No one knows, but every year someone has a new theory, usually right around Halloween something gets published in the campus paper. Whatever is in there, though, it ain't friendly."

"So, has anyone ever killed themselves in the neighboring rooms? Like this one?"

"Nah, just 733. Honestly, I was surprised when I heard they were opening the north hall this year."

"They told us we were the biggest incoming freshman class in twenty years." I said absentmindedly.

"Yeah, I heard that, too. You know you could request a room change." Ian sat down on the bed next to me and I leaned against his shoulder.

"Yeah, but they wouldn't keep us together." Lydia cut in. "Becca and I have been best friends for 15 years. We can't room with other people."

"So should we just keep living here, next to Satan?" I glanced at the closet door again.

Lydia shrugged. "At least we'll have some stories to tell after graduation."

"These aren't the kind of stories I want to tell."

*

A few days later Lydia began to believe my closet story. I woke up in the middle of the night to the sound of someone whispering. I looked over at Lydia, who was already staring at me with wide eyes. She slowly brought a finger to her lips.

I listened intently, trying to hear what the voice was saying and where it was coming from but I couldn't understand even one word. I got out of my bed and tiptoed over to Lydia's. The whispering was definitely louder over there, but then she shared a wall with room 733. I listened harder.

...never...taken...mouths...of fools...

What the hell? Lydia leaned over and put her ear up to the wall. The whispers suddenly stopped and I leaned closer. Suddenly there was a loud bang from the other side. Lydia immediately recoiled and clutched her ear in pain.

Someone was in there. Suddenly more angry than scared I again threw open our door and stomped over to the supposedly empty supply room. I banged on the door loudly not caring who else I woke up at this point.

"Are you fucking kidding me?!" I yelled at the door. "This shit isn't funny anymore. Come out of that fucking room, you asshole."

Silence. And then the doorknob started to turn.

I don't know what I'd expected to happen but it wasn't that. I backed up so far from the door that I ran into the opposite wall. When the handle had turned all the way down, something started to push from the other side. The door groaned loudly but the locks held.

I held my breath until the pressure on the door subsided and the handle slowly returned to its normal position.

I noticed Lydia peaking her head out of our room. She held up her hands as if to say *what happened?*

"Someone thinks they're funny." I answered her out loud. She shook her head and disappeared back into our room.

I knelt down on the floor and brought my head down to the carpet, peering under the door crack. It was the first time I had seen into the corner room.

Room 733 was definitely a supply closet. There were chairs stacked along one wall and bed frames along the other. A few rotting mattresses were piled under one of the windows and a thick layer of dust covered everything in the room. The windows were absolutely huge, which was something you couldn't really tell by looking up at the building. There were open as always and I could definitely see how someone could easily climb through them to the outside ledge.

The room didn't look like it had been disturbed in a couple of decades which sent a shudder wracking through my body.

The moonlight, which had been providing enough light to see into the room, suddenly vanished and I saw only pitch black inside. I blinked rapidly trying to adjust my night vision. I squeezed my eyes shut and when I opened them, a large yellow eye was looking back at me, only a few inches away from my face on the other side of the door.

I screamed and woke up half the dorm.

*

There was no denying that things were escalating. The next morning Lydia and I put in dorm change requests with Resident Services and hoped for the best. In the meantime, we agreed to never be alone in our dorm room at night. Either we both spent the night at home or neither of us did. We started spending most nights with our respective boyfriends.

I told Ian everything that had happened and he suggested I maybe talk to the campus Paranormal Society. I hesitantly made an appointment and Lydia and I met with a small, cleanly dressed kid named Craig and four of his "colleagues" the following Tuesday.

We told them everything we could remember, every incident, no matter how small. Craig and the four other members of the Paranormal Society sat quietly and took notes for half an hour. It wasn't until we finished that anyone spoke.

"Is that all?" Craig asked.

"Yes..." I said slowly.

"Would you mind waiting out in the hall for a few minutes so that I may confer with my colleagues?"

"Sure," Lydia smiled indulgently and stood up. "Whatever you need."

The door had barely shut behind us when Lydia snorted and rolled her eyes. "Let's go."

"Go where?" I asked.

"Are you serious?"

"Lydia, come on, we need help, I am *freaking* out. We haven't stayed one night in our dorm since Thursday so this isn't something we can just brush off."

"Okay." She threw her hands up. "Let's hear what they have to say and then we can go over to Resident Services and check on our move requests."

We loitered out in the hallway for another 15 minutes before Craig came out and asked up to come back and take a seat.

With all the pomp and circumstance of a meeting of parliament, Craig cleared his throat and made his diagnosis.

"What you're dealing with, ladies, is a very angry ghost."

"Is that your professional opinion, Craig?" Lydia said. I shot her a look.

"Y-yes," he stuttered. "A vengeful spirit-"

"A spirit?" I asked. I very much doubted that that's what we were dealing with.

"Yes," answered one of the not-Craigs. "That's ghost to the layperson."

"Jesus Christ," Lydia groaned and rubbed her temples.

Mistaking Lydia's frustration with despair, Craig rushed right into his speech.

"Don't be afraid, ladies, we're going to take care of you. It's true that spirits can be quite a headache if you don't know how to exorcize them which is why it's good you came to us. Suicides almost always result in angry ghosts, they need revenge."

"Revenge on whom?" I asked.

"On other students. Perhaps this particular spirit was bullied into taking his own life and now seeks to torment others."

"Ah, listen-"

"We can take care of this for you right away, all we ask is a small donation to the society," Craig continued. "We honestly didn't realize that room was having this much activity. It's really very exciting."

"Great, well, thank you for your time," Lydia said as she grabbed my hand and pulled me out of my chair.

"Do you want to set something up for this weekend?" Craig asked.

"Tell you what, we'll call you."

Lydia hurried me out of the room wearing a weary look and we didn't speak again until we were almost to the Admin building.

"That was a waste of time." She said.

"Look, I'm not disagreeing with you, but-"

"Becca, tell me you didn't honestly buy into that?"

"So you don't think it's a...a..." I was having trouble even saying the word, it sounded so ridiculous. "...ghost?"

"Well, I don't fucking know, but neither do they. That guy had no idea what the fuck he was talking about."

I pulled my hood lower over my eyes as we stepped into line at the Resident Services desk.

"Let me put it this way." Lydia continued. "They're playing Ghostbusters and we're* living* the fucking Exorcist."

"Fine," I sighed. "Then what do you want to do? Just keep sleeping at Mike and Ian's until we get reassigned?"

"I just want this to end." Lydia crossed her arms and stared straight ahead. We all wanted this to end. Even if living next to that fucking room wasn't scary it was sure as hell distracting.

"Alright, well, I mean we're probably safe during daylight hours so as long as we don't spend nights there we should be okay. Our room is only ghost adjacent after all, and our new assignments will come through soon." I checked my watch. "Fuck it's almost 2."

"Shit, really? I gotta go. Mike got accepted to Sigma Chi and he's getting initiated today."

"Oh yeah, I forgot he rushed."

The girl at the desk waved us forward. I hadn't even realized we'd reached the front of the line.

"Let me know what they say," Lydia said as she ran out the door.

The girl at the desk eyed me suspiciously as I approached.

"Hi, I'm-"

"You're the girl trying to move out of 734 in Reilly, aren't you?"

She'd caught me off guard. "Yeah, one of them. How'd you know?"

"Sorry, I overheard you. I also saw your file cross my desk a few days ago and I gotta ask: why are you looking to transfer rooms, exactly?"

I was tired. I was beaten down. I didn't have the energy to think of a lie.

"Because shit is going on in the empty room next door and it's really freaking us out. Noises, whispers, knocking, the other night I saw someone..."

"You saw someone?"

"Yeah."

"In room 733?"

"Yeah. I looked under the door. There was definitely someone in there."

The girl narrowed her eyes at me for a moment and then nodded for no particular reason.

"Well, your rooms aren't ready yet but I've pushed them through as a priority. For right now you're stuck, though. There just isn't anywhere else to put you."

I sighed. I'd figured as much.

"I'm Alice," she continued, "and, look, I've actually done a lot of research on the Reilly suicides and I think I can help you. Or at the very least offer some insight."

"Really?" I asked, hesitantly.

"Absolutely. I'm in Taylor Hall, room 310. I'll be back to my dorm by 4 today."

"Thanks. We just came from the Paranormal Society on campus."

"Ugh, say no more," Alice rolled her eyes.

"Yeah, so…I'll definitely see you at 4."

"Great," Alice said, and smiled.

*

I was early to Taylor, but then so was she. I told our story for the second time that day and Alice wasn't afraid to interrupt with questions, though her queries didn't betray her thoughts.

When I was finished she leaned back in her chair and sighed deeply.

"I can't believe it," she shook her head. "I'd always heard rumors but I honestly doubted any of it was true."

"I can assure you – everything I've told you is absolutely true."

"And how is it now? When you're there?"

"We aren't ever there at night but during the day we've heard scratching on the wall, really quiet whispering and sometimes we still hear the window opening and closing. In broad fucking daylight. However every time I look up from the street the windows to 733 are open."

101

Alice nodded. "Well, for the record I don't think you're in any danger. As much as it sucks, you guys are simply a casualty. You just need to stay out of room 733."

I snorted. "Are you kidding? I would never go in there."

"I believe that you believe that. But this thing, whatever it is, it's tricky. Manipulative. A *liar*. And it's smarter than you."

"I'll try not to be offended by that."

"You shouldn't be."

"What do you think it is?"

"Something very old and very evil."

I regarded her skeptically and then let my eyes wander around the room. I hadn't really noticed the décor before but to say Alice had an interest in the occult was an understatement.

"I can't see any situation where I would be compelled to enter that room."

"I know. But you have to be prepared that there may come a time when you have to make a *decision* about entering that room. Because what you're dealing with? It's already killed five people."

"Five?! I thought it was three!"

"Yeah, well, not everyone is inclined to do the level of research that I do. Let's see, there was Ellen Burnham in 1961 – she jumped out the window. She was the very first. And then Tad Collinsworth in 1968 - he jumped, too. Marissa Grigg in 1975, she hung herself. Erin Murphy in 1979 - she jumped. And then Erik Dousten in 1992 - he hung himself."

"Five suicides. How could the university still let people live in there?"

"They don't, apparently. That's why it's a supply room."

"And back then?"

"Well, every few years, once everyone who would remember had graduated, the room would be reassigned. This was before the internet, you know, and the incoming freshman were clueless. But after that last one - Erik Dousten - they closed the entire north hall of the 7th floor and built more rooms onto the south hall."

"So, what does it want?"

Alice shrugged. "Chaos. Death. Souls. Who knows? No one even knows what it *is*."

"Okay, so what *do* we know?"

"We know that it's somehow bound to that room though it seems to have minimal influence just outside of it. We know that everyone who ever died was alone at the time. And we know that it's a trickster. That's what we know."

It wasn't enough. "Why do you think they do it?" I asked quietly.

"The victims?"

I nodded.

"All I know is what's rumored to be in the evidence files. All the suicides were found with pictures or writings that were considered 'unspeakable' at the time. They contained horrible, evil things that would make you physically sick to read or see, they say."

"And these people, they drew them? They wrote that stuff?"

"Yep. Whatever is in that room drove them mad."

"That's fucking terrifying."

"Have you guys considered getting somebody to bless the room?"

"Jesus."

"Well you'll have a hard time getting him but perhaps some other sort of holy person."

"No, I mean, Jesus, you're talking about an exorcism."

Alice shrugged. "Maybe. The rumor in the 70s was that this all started with a Ouija board game gone wrong in 1961."

"Really? That shit's made by Hasbro."

"Not in the 60s it wasn't. Anyway, it's just a rumor. The only person on campus who would know is Tom Garris in Admin. I've tried to talk to him before but he refuses to see me."

"Did he go here in 1961?"

"Yes. And he was staying in Reilly."

"We need to talk to him. I need to know what the fuck is happening or I won't be able to live the rest of my life as a well-adjusted person."

"I suppose we can try to chase him down on campus."

"Can we talk to him tomorrow?"

"We can try."

*

Mr. Garris wouldn't see us that day or the next. We tried to catch him on his lunch hour and then again while he was leaving work but he got around us every time. It was soon clear that the old man was actively avoiding us.

Lydia and I had seen little of each other since we'd continued to sleep in other dorms. I went back to our room twice a day - once in the morning and once in the afternoon. Usually the other room was silent but that didn't make me feel better. I could always sense something on the other side of the wall, somehow watching me. It felt like the calm before the storm.

The Thursday before Halloween I came back to the dorm to shower in the evening, much later than usual. I'd seen Lydia that afternoon and she'd informed me that she had enough clothes stored at Mike's to last until graduation so I knew I'd be there alone.

I showered down the hall in the safety of the bathrooms and then walked back to my room to change. I was supposed to meet Ian in half an hour to head out to a party and I wanted to get out of here as quick as possible.

Since the silence was unnerving me, I threw my iPod on the docking station and turned up AC/DC.

I got dressed and then stood in front of the mirror to dry my hair. I flipped my head over and blow dried upside down to try and give my hair some volume. When I flipped my head back up and shut off the blow-dryer I immediately noticed the silence in the room. But that wasn't all I noticed.

I wasn't in my dorm anymore. Behind me was reflected the dusty bedframes and large open windows of room 733. I spun around in a panic to find that I was actually standing in my own room. I looked back at the mirror to see that 733 still reflected there. A slight movement behind me was all it took to make me run.

I grabbed my purse and phone and I fled from my room slamming the door behind me. On the elevator ride down I called Alice.

"I can't do it anymore," I said when she picked up. "I can't go back in that room, again. I can't ever go back."

"What happened?"

I told her.

"Jesus. What do you want to do?" She asked.

"I need to talk to someone who knows what the fuck is going on. Is Tom Garris the only person we know was here in 1961?"

"The only one I know of. Maybe we can get him on his way in tomorrow morning? We'll just corner him and refuse to move until he tells us something. He comes in at 6:30 according to the schedule I have. Do you want to meet me outside the Starbucks in the Atrium?"

"Fuck yeah I do. I have a class at 7:30 but I'll blow it off."

"Okay. See you then."

I wasn't usually much for parties but I was glad I was going to one that night. As soon as we got there I asked Ian to get me a drink. Since I wasn't usually much of a drinker he gave me a raised eyebrow. I gave him a brief synopsis of what had happened earlier, hoping he wouldn't think I was crazy.

Ian made me a scotch and coke. It was the first of many.

Around midnight I went to have a cigarette and checked my phone. I had a voicemail from Lydia left at 11:04pm.

"Hey Becca, listen I just, ugh, I just had a huge fucking fight with Mike. He, well, I guess his frat decided that for Halloween this year all the new brothers have to spend the night in the Suicide Room. In our dorm. I just, I can't fucking take it. He knows what's been going on with us and he still agreed to do this. He's now trying to convince me that Sigma Chi is behind all of the stuff going on in room 733 because they've been trying to drum up buzz for their Halloween deal. I can't-"

I hit end and threw my phone in my bag. No wonder Lydia was pissed. This was not good. Not good at all.

I found Ian inside and asked him to take me home. I was suddenly very stressed, very tired and very drunk.

When the alarm went off at 6am, it took everything I had to pull myself out of bed. I got dressed in the clothes I'd worn the night before and shuffled my way across campus to the Atrium.

Alice was already there with a black coffee in hand.

"I figured you'd need this," she laughed.

"How'd you know?"

"Your texts."

"I texted you last night?"

"Yeah, at about 1. You told me about Sigma Chi."

"Oh, god, yeah." I pushed my sunglasses higher up my nose and pulled my hood lower over my eyes.

"Those guys are idiots. Remember how I told you that it's crafty? Well what if the point of messing with you was to make 733 provocative, you know, to seduce people into going inside. No one has been in that room for years, can you imagine how hungry that thing is?"

"Do you think they're really at risk?" I asked as I sat down on the steps to the Admin building.

"Yeah. In fact the *only* thing they have going for them is that all those suicide victims were alone at the time of their deaths."

"So, it'll be less powerful with all of them there?"

"Theoretically. We would know a lot more if we knew what it was. And we can't know what it is without knowing how it got here. And that is why we need Garris."

"What time is he supposed to get here?"

"Actually, twenty minutes ago," Alice said, grimly.

It was another half an hour before we resigned ourselves to the fact that Mr. Garris had snuck around us as usual. We went to the front office hoping to beg again for an appointment with him anyway.

The woman at the Admin desk regarded us coldly.

"Tom isn't coming in today. Or any other day for that matter. He quit yesterday. Looks like you won't be harassing him anymore."

"We weren't harassing him," I said. "We just desperately needed to talk to him."

"We still do." Added Alice.

"Well you won't get any of his personal information from me," she said snidely and walked away.

"What the fuck do we do now?" I asked Alice.

"Without Tom Garris there's nothing left to do."

"Alice, fuck, I can't go back into that room.

"Well, then I guess it's good your transfers came through."

"They did?!"

"Yep. I got the notice when I checked my work email this morning. You're going to Morton and Lydia is going to Tinsley."

"Oh thank god."

"I thought you'd be happy about that. I also convinced my boss not to assign anyone else to room 734."

"Thank fuck."

"The only thing is you won't be able to move until Monday."

"I can last through the weekend, especially now that the end is in sight. I have to tell Lydia."

I opened my phone to pull up Lydia's number but my attention was caught by the red '1' badge over the voicemail logo. I hit play. It was the rest of the message from last night.

"-even look at his dumb fucking face anymore so I'm going to head home. Don't worry about me, I'll be okay. I'm drunk enough to sleep through any bullshit from next door. I'm just so fucking pissed off right now. I would honestly rather deal with Dumbshit Beth than Michael-My-Parents-Must-Be-Siblings-Because- I'm-That-Fucking-Retarded-Benson. Let's hang out tomorrow. Love ya!"

The message ended.

"Goddamn it."

Alice gave me a questioning look.

"Lydia spent the night in our dorm."

Alice cringed.

"She's safe though, right?"

"As long as she doesn't go into 733."

"She won't." I thought of the always open large windows of the corner room. If nothing else the mere thought of those would keep Lydia the hell out of that room.

"Good. Well, since we have nothing else to do, do you want to go look for theology books in the library? It's pretty much the only thing open right now. "

"Sure," I shrugged. I didn't have another class until 10.

The little old lady who sat behind the library's checkout desk must have been 1,000 years old. Ms. Stapley's eyes were small and watery and her skin looked like it was melting off of her skull. Still, she was nice and knowledgeable and she sent us in the right direction for books on demonology, though she gave us a curious look as she did.

There wasn't much. We read everything we could but it either wasn't relevant or wasn't in English. We returned to her desk 30 minutes later.

"Ah, do you have anything on the occult?"

"The occult? Ah..." Her voice trailed off. "Yes, I do. Over there to the left of the reference section."

"Ok thanks. Sorry, I'm too hung-over to use the Dewey decimal system," I said.

"I don't think she likes the look of us," Alice whispered as we walked away.

"Our look or our subject matter?"

"Probably neither."

Within the hour we were back up at her desk having struck out again. We could tell she was getting annoyed as her eyes narrowed suspiciously at us as we approached.

"Ah, sorry, do you know where we could find something on séances or Ouija boards or-"

"Now listen, girls." Ms. Stapley stood up from her desk and looked over her glasses at us. "I really hope this is for class."

"It is," I said.

"It's not," Alice answered simultaneously. "It's personal research."

"Research? What kind of research?"

"Look, we're not going to mess with a Ouija board or anything..." I said.

"Good," Ms. Stapley smoothed her pleated pants and sat back down. "Because I can't have that sort of thing going on here again."

"*Again?*" Alice latched on.

The older woman suddenly looked very uncomfortable and started fidgeting with a stack of books on her desk.

"We may have something on séances in-"

"Ms. Stapley, we're researching what happened in Reilly in 1961." Alice interrupted.

"And also what's been happening there ever since."

"Well, it's no secret, is it? A student committed suicide in that room. Dreadful but not unheard of on a university campus."

"Five students." I corrected her.

"But you know that, right?" Alice was suddenly talking very fast. "Because you sound like you're well versed in this story. Please, tell us how this started and we might be able to end it."

"End it?" Ms. Stapley's voice became quieter but more concentrated. "Don't be so arrogant, young lady. You can't end it. People have always died in that room and they always will. There is no end to it so you'd best stay far away from it."

"But maybe if we knew how this all started -"

"It started just as you think it did. But everyone that was involved is either very old or very dead by now. Just stay away from that room. Concentrate on your studies."

I leaned over her desk. "Well, I'd love to but they assigned my friend and me to the room next door. Maybe you can forget about all the suicides but we can't. It won't fucking let us."

"Young lady, I never forget." Ms. Stapely voice was even quieter now. "My friend Ellen was the very first to be killed in that room. She was my very best friend and not a night goes by that I don't imagine her wiggling out of that tiny window, standing upon the cold ledge in her bare feet and jumping off the 7th floor of that building."

Alice sighed. "I'm really sorry. I didn't know."

"Yes, well these are old wounds, my dear. Now girls, I suggest you request a room reassignment immediately. No one should be living on the seventh floor of that building. And that's all I'm going to tell you about it. "

Alice sighed but resigned herself to a nod. We wouldn't learn anything more here. Still, it was quite a breakthrough - at least we had *some* information now.

Alice walked away and I made to follow her but my feet wouldn't move. Something was bothering me - a small yet poignant word had been buried in Ms. Stapley's story; a word that suddenly seemed very important.

"Eh, Ms. Stapley," I asked the tired, old woman at the desk, "Why did you refer to the windows in 733 tiny? Because I've seen those windows and they're huge, like 5 feet tall."

"Dear, you're thinking of the corner room, that's the supply closet. Room 733 is next door to that."

"No-no," I stuttered, "that's room 734."

"Yes, well, it is *now*. When they built the additional rooms on to the south hall they moved all the room numbers down."

Oh my god. I suddenly felt very hot and very dizzy.

"That sneaky fucker," Alice whispered next to me, her skin paling.

"Lydia."

We took off across the campus at a dead run, witnessed only by the few bleary-eyed students on their way to morning classes. When Reilly finally came into view I stumbled on the pavement as my blood turned to ice. From our vantage point we could clearly see the windows of the corner room were closed – the first and only time I had ever seen that way. And the window to my room was open.

We ran into the lobby, pushing past several latte-sipping, Ugg boot-wearing freshman who had just gotten off the elevator. I hit 7 and watched the doors close more slowly than they ever had before. I leaned against the wall, trying to steady my breathing.

"Alice, how the fuck did this happen?"

"I don't know. I don't fucking know."

"She's been in there all night, Alice. In our room. Alone."

Alice shook her head but had nothing to say.

When the doors finally opened on floor 7, we saw a quiet, deserted hallway. I ran toward my room with Alice right behind me. Rounding the corner, I threw open my door hoping it wasn't locked. And it wasn't.

Lydia looked back at me. And for one breathless moment, cruel glimmer of hope crossed over her tear streaked face.

But it was too late. The next second, she leaned forward so slightly, and she was gone.

She screamed the entire way down.

Alice ran to the ledge where Lydia had just been while I stood motionless. She stuck her head out the window and looked down just as a different kind of screaming started from the bottom floor. Alice closed her hand over her mouth and pulled her head back into the room as tears of shock ran down her ghost- white face.

The screaming from outside got louder as more people saw what remained of my best friend on the cold pavement. I leaned back against the dresser and slumped to the floor. A falling death. Lydia never wanted a falling death.

I absentmindedly picked up one of the pictures that were strewn all over the floor. It was a picture of Lydia's mother. She was dead. I picked up another picture. It was Lydia's baby sister. She was dead, too. There were dozens of pictures just like it all over the floor - Lydia has been busy last night. As for the things depicted in them, I cannot tell you. Lydia was a talented artist and I only saw a few before I got sick on the floor next to me.

Alice was standing in the doorway yelling something down the hall. I don't know what she was saying because all I could hear was a high pitched whine in the room. Suddenly a piece of paper slid out from under the crack in the closet door and glided across the floor toward me. I picked it up and studied it for a moment.

This was drawn by Lydia too, but it wasn't like the others. It was a picture of the closet from my exact vantage point. In the drawing the door was cracked and there was something looking back from the darkness.

I put the paper down and studied the closet. The door was cracked open just like the picture. I squinted my eyes and tried to see inside. Just as I started to distinguish the defined lines of a long face looking back at me, Alice pulled me to my feet.

"We need to get out of here," I thought I heard her say.

I never went back into that room. My parents moved my things and I spent the rest of the semester in an apartment off campus. I transferred to an out of state school for my spring semester and finished my degree there.

Every night I dream of Lydia pulling herself through the tiny window, shimmying out onto the cold ledge, standing up and knowing there's nothing between her body and the terrifying abyss in front of her. I watch her look down seven stories to the black pavement below and realize, though not accept, her terrible fate. I see the blind horror cross her familiar features. I hear her wildly pounding heart, desperately trying to race through every beat of the life she should have lived, and knowing it has only mere seconds.

I watch her look back at me. And I watch her fall.

It's been 9 years since that night. And every fall semester for 9 years I've called Resident Services to see which dorms are open for new student assignments. Reilly is always open. The seventh floor is closed.

This year life and work got in the way and I called much later than usual. I was put on hold immediately.

"Resident Services." A man finally answered. "Were you the one asking about open rooms in Reilly?"

"Yes, that's me."

"We're entirely filled up and there's a waiting list for Reilly. But, as it happens, you actually have great timing. I make no promises but we may be able to get you in. We just got approval this morning."

"Approval for what?" I asked dubiously.

"We're opening up the seventh floor."

PALEONTOLOGISTS WERE WE

Jake was my best friend when I was a kid. We'd bonded over a deep obsession of the Jurassic Park movies and our resulting passion for Paleontology.

We used to spend every weekend out in the woods excavating the forest floor for dinosaur bones.

But one day when we came home from school and gathered up our digging equipment, my parents stopped us on the way out the door. They told us it wasn't safe to go outside today. We went up to my room but we could still hear the adults whispering about "another body being found after all these years".

Jake's parents came over and they sat us down in the living room and made us promise to only play in our backyards from now on. We insisted we weren't *playing*, we were making scientific discoveries. They just smiled at Jake and me and sent us outside with squirt guns, which we abandoned as soon as we were out the door. I snuck up to my room and grabbed our tools instead.

That was the day we finally hit pay dirt. After a year and a half of excavating we had finally found our first section of dinosaur skeleton – and in my backyard no less! We hurried inside to tell our parents but they had left to a neighborhood meeting and only my father was home. When we told him he was very excited and agreed to take us to the university the next afternoon to present our findings to the anthropology department for testing.

But we never went to the university. And it wasn't because my dad didn't keep his promise, either. It was because Jake never made it home from school the next day. And he never came home any other day either. I was scared and lonely for a few months but my parents hired me a therapist and I slowly got better. By the time we moved out of state less than a year later, I'd forgotten entirely about the dinosaur bones we had discovered in the back yard.

Until today.

This morning my daughter came home from a weekend with Grandma and Grandpa. She said she hadn't been allowed to go outside because of some missing kids in the area. And for the first time since I was nine I thought about the bones Jake and I found in my backyard. And I wondered...

Walker

THE SUICIDE OF BRADLEY ALLIGAN

Bradley Alligan died on a quiet Wednesday morning in August of
1999.

By all accounts Bradley was a happy, healthy, well-adjusted 29
year old man. He was a biology professor at a local community
college living with his girlfriend, Megan, and their five year old son.
Megan had still been asleep when two cops knocked on her door a
few minutes before 9am.

"What is your name?"

"Megan Owens...is something wrong?"

"Do you know a person named Bradley Alligan?"

"Yes."

"Would you like to sit down?"

The officers explained that the body of a man had been seen
falling from Cold Spring Canyon Arch Bridge just after sunrise that
morning. The witness called police. Bradley's car was found parked
on the bridge with a running video camera positioned on his dash
board recording his final minutes.

"Oh my God... And did you, did you watch the recording?"

"Yes, ma'am, we did."

"And did he...j- jump?"

"Yes, Ma'am."

This was the detail that Megan would suffer from most in her
life. After the shock had passed and the grief had built and peaked
and finally cooled to a tolerable ache, after years had separated Megan
from that traumatic morning...she never let it go. This one detail was
sour to her, it was absurd and inconsistent with Stephen's character.
Why record your own death?

Was it because he wanted her to know, without a doubt, that
he'd done it to himself? Did he do it because he knew no one would
believe he was capable of suicide and he wanted to avoid exhaustive
investigations for his family's sake? Had he been trying to actually
record something else and had fallen over the railing and into the
gorge?

After the ME had officially ruled cause of death to be suicide
Megan asked for Bradley's body back. His family intervened and took

custody of it, opting to cremate their son and spread his ashes over their rural farm. Megan was in no legal position to stop them.

So when the cops offered Megan the tape she took it, though they stressed to her that the tape should be destroyed.

She didn't destroy the tape, but she didn't watch it either. Instead, she obsessed over it.

The little 8mm drove her slowly insane. Megan spent the last decade of her life trying to understand Bradley's state of mind on the day of his death. She studied his notes, interviewed his friends and colleagues, she made graphs and spreadsheets and suffered horrific nightmares while she tried to make sense of that day.

But she still never watched the tape.

And then, one day, she went missing. I was sixteen at the time and had been staying at my friend's house over the weekend. I thought it was weird that she wasn't there when I came home but I was happy about it. My mom was quiet and moody and we really didn't seem to have anything in common, though we got along alright. She told me I was more like my father. I don't think she liked that about me.

So I was happy to be given an extra reprieve from her negativity. When she still wasn't back when I got home from school on Tuesday I started to worry. I spent most of that night debating whether or not I should call the police.

I didn't, and early the next morning they showed up at my door anyway.

"What is your name?"

"Robby Alligan."

"Is your mother Megan Owens?"

"She-she's missing."

"Is that your mom?"

"Yes."

"When did you last see her?"

"Friday morning. Well, last Friday morning. It was before school. But I've been gone since then, I mean I got back on Sunday but her car was gone so-"

"It's alright, will you take a seat?"

They told me she was found in the gorge by some hikers. They said her car was parked on the shoulder of the road next the Arch

Bridge. They asked if she had been depressed lately and also if I knew anyone who'd wanted to hurt her. I said no.

One cop went outside to make a phone call and the other asked me to go upstairs and pack some things, asked if I had family nearby. Only my dad's family, who lived on a farm, who I'd never met.

I packed a bag and then I went into my mom's room to grab the tape that had meant so much to her. I couldn't leave it behind.

I wasn't surprised to find it in our old VCR. Somehow I knew, if she was dead - she'd watched the tape.

The TV screen was blue with the bold, white letters of PLAY flashing in the upper right-hand corner.

I'd always respected my mom's wishes in regard to the tape. Though I was insanely curious about my dad I never watched it, never snuck into her room to so much as touch it, though I'd always known where she hid it. But now I wanted to know what she'd seen. I *had* to know. Whatever was on that tape had killed both of my parents and I was feeling no emotion about their deaths. I was just...numb. Was I in shock? Or was there something wrong with me? I knew the tape held my answers.

I rewound the cassette back 3 minutes. Then I hit *PLAY*.

The screen blinked a second and then I was looking at an empty bridge and a concrete railing to the right. There was nothing on the other side of the barrier but dimly lit sky. It was also drizzling lightly, which is something I hadn't known about that day. The POV was through the windshield of a car, like a modern day dashcam.

There were no people in the shot. I hadn't gone back far enough.

I hit *STOP* and then *REWIND*. I let it go back another twenty minutes and then I hit *PLAY* again.

This time, the camera was moving, or rather, the car was. The only sounds were the hum of the highway, the pitter-patter of rain on the windshield and my father's ragged breathing. After a few minutes I could hear another sound as well - quiet crying.

I could see the bridge approaching from a distance and by the time he pulled up to it, his breathing was even and the crying had stopped. My father parked the car on the side of the bridge and rolled all the windows down. Then he got out and I heard the sound of the backdoor opening and a rustling behind the camera.

When he re-emerged at the front of the car, he was dragging something behind him. He stopped to address the camera and spun the thing around to face it. It was a little boy.

A cold shudder wracked through my body as I recognized my five year old self. I'd been there that day? I'd seen my father die? I remembered nothing of it. I hugged my arms to my body and turned the volume up as my father began to talk to the camera.

"What did you do, Megan? We were a family, we loved each other. We were happy."

As he spoke I watched my little face on the screen. Instead of looking scared or confused or uncomfortable, I was smiling. It was the smile of a child who'd gotten away with stealing a cookie from the cupboard, or quietly staying up late playing video games after bedtime.

"I've tried it dozens of times. I've used controls, lab equipment from the school, I've taken meticulous notes, and I've destroyed it all because the result is always the same. He *always* comes back."

Then, he lifted the child up into his arms and five year old me stared into the camera.

"It's not natural, it's not right." I could hear the emotion creeping into his voice. I couldn't tell for certain in the rain but I was sure he was crying.

"He always comes back." His voice cracked and the child on screen picked up his head and started laughing at him. My father's face registered fear and then he took two determined steps to the concrete railing and then threw me over the side of the bridge. The laughing didn't stop once I was thrown over, just faded down into the abyss with me as I fell.

I stumbled away from the TV and fell onto my mom's bed. What the fuck?! How did I survive a fall from a 400 foot tall bridge? I took quick, unnecessary, stock of my familiar body to see if I could find any scars, phantom pains, or permanent damage.

When I finally looked back at the screen my father was staring out of it, looking directly at me as if he'd been waiting for my attention.

"What did you do Megan?" His voice was so quiet I barely heard it.

"What did you DO?" He yelled this last sentence and then made them his final words by walking over the side of the bridge, throwing his leg over the railing and then sort of just rolling off the ledge.

The rest of the tape was what I'd seen earlier: the sky lightening and the rain letting up. And then the tape just ended. I never watched it again.

I spent the next year living on my grandparent's farm, doing every drug I could get a hold of in their small town. Toward the end of my time there I sobered up just long enough to track down the cops who'd responded to my dad's suicide.

Of the three who had watched the tape, only one remained on the force. I bombarded his office with calls that he never responded to. I was debating giving up when a letter arrived in the mail for me. It was from the officer, a detective now. He asked me to stop calling his office and to please never contact him again. He'd wanted nothing to do with me then and even less so now. It was a polite letter and he did answer my question.

Your father's body was the only one found under the bridge. When we went to inform your mother that her husband was dead and her son missing, we found you sleeping peacefully in bed. How can we charge a dead man with the murder of a boy whose body is still breathing? We walked away from this case.

Although I'm too afraid to continue my father's experiments, I have had some confirmation that I would get the same results. During one of my more intense binges I did enough heroine to kill ten Keith Richards. But I woke up fine. And then last year I was in a car accident that reduced my truck to two square meters of twisted metal. The cops found me dazed, sitting next to the wreckage - my clothes coated in my own blood and torn to shreds. But I didn't have a scratch on me.

Sometimes I sober up just long enough for the clouds to part and clarity to descend. I remember more of my childhood in these moments, and I remember further back than I should. Lost memories resurface like whales from the depths of the ocean, breaking the surface so briefly and then sinking back into the abyss.

I remember how much my parents loved each other. I remember how much they loved me. I can see my mother smiling; I'd never seen her smile before. I remember the sickness too, sometimes. Laying in my warm bed at home for months and then laying in the cold one at the hospital. But then another memory lapse in and I'm outside playing, just your average healthy three year old. And then I remember my father on the tape, confused and scared and desperate.

"What did you do, Megan?"

BORRASCA
PART 1

It's a long story, but one you've never heard before. This story is about a place that dwells on the mountain; a place where bad things happen. And you may think you know about the bad things, you may decide you have it all figured out but you don't. Because the truth is worse than monsters or men.

At first I was upset when they told me we were moving to some little town out in the Ozarks. I remember staring at my dinner plate while I listened to my sister throw a temper tantrum unbefitting of a 14 year old honors student. She cried, she pleaded, and then she cursed at my parents. She threw a bowl at my dad and told him it was all his fault. Mom told Whitney to calm down but she stormed off, slamming every door in the house on the way to her room.

I secretly blamed my dad as well. I'd heard the whispers too, my dad had done something wrong, something bad and the sheriff's department had reassigned him to some little out of the way county to save face. My parents didn't want me to know that, but I did.

I was nine so it didn't take me too long to warm to the idea of a change; it was like an adventure. New house! New school! New friends! Whitney, of course, felt the opposite. Moving to a new school at her age is hard, moving away from her new boyfriend, however, was even harder. While the rest of us packed up our things and said our goodbyes, Whitney sulked and cried and threatened to run away from home. But a month later when we pulled up to our new house in Drisking, Missouri she was sitting right next me texting viciously on her phone.

Thankfully, we moved over the summer and I had months of free time to explore the town. When Dad started his new job at the sheriff's office, Mom drove us around the city commenting on this and that. The city was much, much smaller than St. Louis but also a lot nicer. There were no 'bad' areas and the entire town looked like something you'd see on a post card. Drisking was built in a mountain valley surrounded by healthy forest land with walking trails and crystal clear lakes. I was 9, it was summer and this was in heaven.

We'd only been living in Drisking a week or so when our next door neighbors came to introduce themselves: Mr. and Mrs. Landy and their 10 year old son Kyle. While our parents talked and drank mimosas, I watched the Landy's lanky, red-headed son hung out in the doorway, shyly eyeing the PS2 in the living room.

"Uh, do you play?" I asked.

He shrugged. "Not really."

"Do you wanna? I just got Tekken 4."

"Um…" Kyle glanced at his mom, who had just been handed her third mimosa. "Yeah. Sure."

And that afternoon, with the ease and simplicity of our age, Kyle and I became best friends. We spent the cool summer mornings outside exploring the Ozarks and the hot afternoons in my living room playing the PS2. He introduced me to the only other kid in the neighborhood our age: a skinny, quiet girl named Kimber Destaro. She was shy but friendly and always up for anything. Kimber kept up with us so well that she quickly became the third wheel on our tricycle.

With my dad at work all the time, my mom consumed with her new friendships and my sister locked in her room all day, the summer was ours to take and take it we did. Kyle and Kimber showed me where all the best hiking trails were, which lakes were the best (and most accessible by bike), and where the best stores were in town. By the time the first day of school rolled around in September I knew I was home.

On the last Saturday before school started, Kyle and Kimber told me they were going to take me somewhere special, somewhere we hadn't been yet – the Triple Tree.

"What's a 'triple tree'?" I asked.

"It's a totally awesome, totally huge treehouse out in the woods." Kyle said excitedly.

"Pfft, whatever, Kyle. Come on, you guys, if there was a freakin' treehouse you would have showed it to me already."

"Na-uh, we wouldn't've," Kyle shook his head. "There's a ceremony for first-timers and everything."

Kimber nodded eagerly in agreement, her dark orange curls bouncing off of her tiny shoulders. "Yep, it's true Sam. If you enter the treehouse without the proper ceremony you'll disappear and then you'll die."

My face fell. Now I knew they were making fun of me. "That's a lie! You guys are lying to me!"

"No we're not!" Kimber insisted.

"Yeah, we'll show you! We just have to get a knife for the ceremony and we'll go."

"What? Why do you need a knife? Is it a blood ceremony?" I whispered.

"No way!" Kimber promised. "You just say some words and carve your name into the Triple Tree."

"Yup, it takes like one minute." Kyle agreed.

"And it's a really cool treehouse?" I asked.

"Oh yeah." Kyle promised.

"Okay, I guess I'll do it then."

Kyle insisted on using the same knife he used during his own ceremony but we paid a price to get it. Mrs. Landy just happened to be home with her youngest son Parker and despite Kyle's many objections his mother insisted he take his six year old brother with him.

"Mom, we're going to the treehouse, it's only for older kids. Parker can't go!"

"I don't care if you're going to see an Exorcist movie marathon, you're taking your brother with you. I need a break, Kyle, can't you understand that? And I'm sure your friends won't mind." She flashed Kimber and me a challenging look. "Right?"

"No, not at all," Kimber said and I nodded in agreement.

Kyle made a loud, dramatic sigh and called his brother. "Parker, put your shoes on, we're leaving now!"

I'd met the youngest Landy several times before and found that he was as unlike his older brother in looks as in disposition. Where Kyle was a wild, excitable fireball with hair to match, I found Parker to be an anxious, fidgety boy with small eyes and dark brown hair.

We got on our bikes and made our way to a lesser known hiking trail a few miles away. I'd asked before where the trail led when we'd ridden across it several weeks before and Kyle had given me the underwhelming answer of "nowhere interesting".

We pulled up to trail head and leaned our bikes against the wooden sign post which read "West Rim Prescott Ore Trail".

"Why are so many trails around here named Prescott?" I asked. "Is this Prescott Mountain or something?"

Kimber laughed. "No, dummy, it's because of *the* Prescott's. You know, the family that lives in the mansion up on Fairmont. Mr. Prescott and his son Jimmy own like half the businesses in town."

"*More* than half," Kyle agreed.

"Which ones? Does he own the Game Stop?" The only store in Drisking I really cared about.

"I don't know about that one," Kyle wound a lock around the 4 bikes and clicked the bar into place, then spun the numbers on the dial. "But like the hardware store, the pharmacy, Gliton's on 2nd and the newspaper."

"Did they start this town?" I asked.

"Nah, mining started the town. I think they-"

"I want to go home." Parker had been so quiet I'd completely forgotten he was there.

"You can't go home," Kyle rolled his eyes. "Mom said I had to bring you. Now come on, it's only like a two mile walk."

"I wanna take my bike." Parker answered.

"Too bad, we're going off trail."

"I don't wanna go. I'll stay with the bikes."

"Don't be such a wussy."

"I'm not!"

"Kyle, be nice!" Kimber hissed. "He's only 5."

"I'm 6!" Parker objected.

"I'm sorry, 6. You're 6." Kimber smiled at him.

"Alright fine, he can hold your hand if he wants. But he's coming." Kyle turned and started up the trail.

Parker's face fell into an undignified frown but when the charming Kimber stuck her hand out and wiggled her fingers at him, he took it.

Kyle was right, it wasn't a long walk – only a half mile down the trail and then another half mile hike on a well tread path up the mountain. It was a steep climb though, and by the time we got to the treehouse, I was winded.

"What do you think?" Kyle asked excitedly.

"It's..." I studied the tree as I caught my breath. "It's pretty awesome," I smiled. And it was. They hadn't lied to me, the treehouse was the biggest one I'd ever seen. It had multiple rooms and there were actual curtains in the windows. A sign above the door said 'Ambercot Fort' and a rope ladder hung below the threshold, missing several planks.

"I'm going up first!" Yelled Parker, but Kimber caught his arm.

"You have to do the ceremony first or you'll disappear." She reminded him.

"That'd be fine with me," Kyle grumbled.

I was eager to get into the fort myself. "Give me the knife." I held out my hand and Kyle smiled and dug the switchblade out of his pocket.

"There's some space in the back to carve your name."

I opened up the knife and walked around the tree looking for an empty spot. They were so many names on the trunk that I had to crunch down and look search near the bottom since I couldn't reach any higher. I spotted both Kyle and Kimber's carvings on the tree and I found a spot I liked near the latter. I bit my tongue and carved *Sam W.* into a blank piece of bark underneath someone named Phil S. Parker went next but had so much trouble with the knife that Kyle ended up doing it for him.

"Alright, let's go," I ran over to the rope ladder.

"Wait!" Kyle yelled. "You have to say the words first."

"Oh yeah. What are they?"

Kimber sang them out. "Underneath the Triple Tree there is a man who waits for me and should I go or should I stay my fate's the same either way."

"That's...creepy." I said. "What does it mean?"

Kimber shrugged. "No one knows anymore, it's just tradition."

"Okay, can you say it one more time, slower?"

Once Parker and I had managed to recite the poem without forgetting the words we were ready to go. I climbed the rope ladder first and took stock of my new surroundings. The treehouse was more or less empty, just a dirty rug here and there and some trash: old soda cans, beer cans and fast food wrappers.

I went room to room – four in total – and found nothing of real interest until I entered the last one. An old mattress lay in the corner and piles of musty, ripped clothing scattered the floor.

"Did a hobo live here?" I asked.

"Nah, this room has been like this for as long as I can remember." Kyle said from the doorway behind me.

"It smells gross." I said.

Kimber walked up to the threshold but refused to go any further. "It's not the smell that freaks me out - it's that." She pointed up to the ceiling and I raised my eyes to read what was written there.

Road to the Gates of Hell
Mile Marker 1

"What does that mean?" I asked.

"It's just older kids being dicks," Kyle said. "Come on, I'll show you the best part of the treehouse."

We walked back into the first room and Parker looked up at us and smiled, pointing down to what he'd clumsily carved into the wooden floor.

"Fart," Kyle read. "That's hilarious, Parker." He rolled his eyes and his little brother smiled proudly.

Kimber sat down on the floor next to Parker and I sat on his other side. Kyle took the knife from his brother and then walked across the room and wedged the blade between two planks of the wooded wall. He applied a slight pressure and the board gave, opening up a small, secret compartment in the wall. Kyle took something out and pushed the plank back in until it was again flush with the wall.

"Check it out." He turned around and proudly held up two cans of Miller Lite beer.

"Whoa!" I said.

"Ewww, warm beer? That's gross. How did you even know it was there?" Kimber asked.

"Phil Saunders told me."

"Are we gonna drink it?" I asked.

"Hell yeah we're gonna drink it!"

Kyle came and sat down in our circle, popped open the first beer and offered it to Kimber. She recoiled as if he was trying to hand her a dirty diaper.

"Come on, Kimmy."

"Don't call me that!" She yelled at him and then reluctantly took the open beer. She smelled it and made a face, then pinched her nose and took a small swig. Kimber shuddered. "That was even grosser than I imagined."

"I don't want any! I'll tell mom!" Parker said quickly as the beer passed in front of him.

"Good, 'cause you ain't getting any," Kyle promised. "And you won't tell mom shit."

I put on my best poker face and took a long, deep swallow of the warm beer before I had the chance to smell it. It was a poor decision and when I wretched, the foul yellow liquid went all over my shirt.

"Aww man, now I'm gonna smell like beer."

We spent the next hour and a half drinking the two cans of Miller Lite and after a while the taste seemed to grow more tolerable. I couldn't tell if I was becoming a man or actually getting drunk. I hoped it was the former. When the last drop of the last beer was consumed we spent 20 minutes trying to determine if we were drunk. Kyle assured us that he was wasted while Kimber wasn't sure. I didn't think I was, but I failed all of our makeshift drunk tests.

Kimber was in the middle of reciting the alphabet backwards when a loud, metallic grinding suddenly pierced the balmy mountain air like a gunshot. Kimber stopped talking and we spent a few minutes staring at each other, waiting for the noise to end. Parker curled into Kimber and put his hands over his ears. After what seemed like ten whole minutes the sound ended as suddenly as it had begun.

"What *was* that?" I asked and Parker mumbled something into Kimber's t-shirt.

"Do you guys know?" I tried again.

Kimber stared at her Keds as she crossed and uncrossed her feet.

"Well?"

"It's nothing," Kyle answered finally. "We hear it sometimes in town, it's not a big deal. It's just louder up here."

"But what's making that sound?"

"Borrasca." Kimber whispered without taking her eyes off her Keds.

"Who's that?" I asked.

"Not who - where." Kyle answered. "It's a place."

"Another town?"

"No, just a place in the woods."

"Oh."

"Bad things happen there," Kimber said more to herself than anyone else.

"Like what?"

"Bad things." Kimber repeated.

"Yeah, don't ever try to find it, dude." Kyle said behind me. "Or bad things will happen to you, too."

"But like, what bad things?" Kyle shrugged and Kimber stood up and walked over to the rope ladder.

"We'd better go. I have to get home to my mom," she said.

We climbed down the ladder one by one and then started the walk back to the trail head in an unfamiliar silence. I was dying of curiosity about Borrasca but couldn't decide if and what to ask about it.

"So, who lives there?"

"Where?" Kyle asked.

"Borrasca."

"The Skinned Men," Parker answered. "And the Shiny Gentleman."

"Pfft," Kyle laughed. "Only babies believe that."

"Like men who are skinned? Like their skin is gone?" I asked excitedly.

"Yeah, that's what some kids say. Most of us stop believing in that, though, when we turn double digits." Kyle said and shot an exasperated look at Parker.

I looked back at Kimber for confirmation but she was still staring down the trail ignoring us. That seemed to be the end of the conversation and by the time we reached our bikes the awkwardness had abated and we were giggling as we tried to decide if we were too drunk to bike home.

School started two days later and by that time I'd completely forgotten about Borrasca. When my dad pulled up to the curb to drop me off that morning he locked the doors before I could get out.

"Not so fast," he laughed. "As your father I get the privilege of giving you a hug and telling you to have a good first day of school."

"But Dad, I gotta go meet Kyle by the flag before first bell!"

"And you will, but give me a hug first. In a few years you'll be driving yourself to school, let me be your dad while I still can."

"Fine." I said and leaned over to give my dad a quick hug.

"Thank you. Now go meet Kyle. Your mom will be waiting here to pick you up at 3:40."

"I *know*, Dad. Why can't I take the bus like Whitney?"

"When you're 13, you can take the bus." He smiled and unlocked the doors. "Until then, I get to drop you off in the mornings. If you think it'd make you look cooler you can ride in the back seat behind the cage."

"Dad...just don't." I threw open the door of his cruiser before he could say anything more and slammed the door on his amused laughter.

Kyle was already waiting for me at the flag pole with Kimber looking around nervously. "Dude, you almost missed the bell!" He yelled when he saw me.

"I know, sorry."

"Whose class are you in?" Kimber asked. She was wearing a red sweater and leggings with frogs on them. Her curly orange hair was brushed into ringlets and her lips were pink and shiny. She'd never looked more feminine and I was surprised to realize I'd never really seen Kimber as a girl.

"Ah, Mr. Diamond's."

"Me too!" She said cheerfully.

"Lucky," Kyle scoffed. "I'm in Mrs. Tverdy's. Only two 6th grade teachers and I get the crappy one."

Kimber grimaced. "Yeah, my mom had her when she was a kid."

"What's wrong with her? What did your mom say?"

"Just that she's strict and gives out homework on the weekends."

"On the *weekends*? Fuck!"

"Excuse me, Mr. Landy?" I immediately recognized the tall man that had suddenly appeared behind the white-faced Kyle.

"So-Sorry, sir. I meant 'dang'."

Kimber giggled.

"I'm sure you did." He nodded.

"Hi, Sheriff Clery." Even though I'd only met him a few times I liked my dad's boss and I think he liked me.

"Well hello, Sammy, are you excited for your first day?" Sheriff Clery crossed his arms in front of him and widened his stance imposingly, but gave me a wide smile.

"Yes sir!" I said. And then added lamely, "What are you doing here?"

"I'm giving a presentation to the 3rd and 4th graders about safety when walking to and from school."

"Yeah, he gives it every year." Kyle muttered.

"Cool," I smiled.

Sheriff Clery nodded at me and then turned and walked away. I turned to Kimber to find an empty space that smelled slightly of strawberries. "Where's Kimber?"

"She took off. She is annoyingly on time to everything." And as if to illustrate his point, the bell rang. We both ran up the stairs and inside the doors.

I walked into class and smiled when I saw that Kimber had saved me a spot next to her at the back. Mr. Diamond, a short, round man of 40 or so nodded at me when I came in.

"Mr. Walker, I presume?"

"Um, yeah, that's me." I mumbled as I rushed past him to the desk next to Kimber.

"Welcome to Drisking Elementary. And for the rest of you, welcome back. Go Grizzlies!"

The class echoed a reluctant and subdued "go grizzlies".

Throughout the morning Kimber introduced me to the other kids in our class. Most of them were nice, if sort of underwhelmed by me. They said their hellos and asked where I was from and the conversations usually ended with an unimpressed "okay".

A group of girls who sat near the front, snuck looks at us all morning and snickered to themselves. I asked Kimber who they were and she just shrugged. During our second break they managed to accost me at the pencil sharpener.

"Are you friends with Kimber Destaro?" A tall, dark-haired girl asked me.

"Yeah," I answered and looked over at Kimber. She was watching me with worried eyes.

"Are you related to her?"

"No."

"I didn't think so because you don't have orange hair." I didn't know what to say to that.

"You don't have to be friends with her, you know," said the second girl with the oddly round face.

"I wanna be friends with her."

A third girl lurking behind the other two snorted. She had pretty auburn hair and a rude, upturned nose.

"Well, if you do you're going to be very unpopular here," the first girl warned. "And once you're in that group you can't ever leave it."

"Better than the bitch group." I said. Rude Nose and Round Face gasped but Dark Hair smiled.

"We'll see," she said and the three returned to their corner of the class room and continued whispering to each other. I sat back down next to Kimber and continued what I'd been writing as if nothing had happened.

"What did they say to you?" Kimber asked nervously.

"They said you're too pretty to be near them and that you make them look ugly in comparison. They'd like us to stay away from them."

"Liar," Kimber answered, but I could hear the smile in her voice.

We met Kyle in the cafeteria at lunch and listened to him artfully complain about his morning. Mrs. Tverdy was ancient and cruel and she'd made every kid in class stand up and say something about themselves even though her room consisted of only 14 kids who'd all known each other since pre-school.

When the bell rang for recess Kyle and I walked over to throw our lunches away. I threw the tray on top of the can and turned around slamming into some kid I'd never seen before.

"Oh, sorry," I mumbled as Kyle laughed at me.

"Wait, are you Sam Walker?" The kid asked.

"Yeah."

"Oh. Your sister is dating my brother."

"Oh man!" Kyle laughed. "Your sister is dating a Whitiger!"

"Shut up, Kyle." The kid snapped.

"She's gonna be Whitney Whitiger!"

As funny as it was I couldn't help but be a little surprised. Not that I'd been paying much attention but I'd only seen Whitney out of her room a couple of times over the entire summer.

"Um, where did she meet him?" I asked the Whitiger kid.

"I dunno. Probably at his job."

"His job where?"

"He works at Drisking Water."

It didn't make any sense to me but I shrugged it off. I did remember my mom giving Whitney some menial tasks like getting the car washed and setting up some utilities to get her out of the house. Maybe she met him once and they started dating over text. Teenagers were weird.

The rest of the school week followed much like the first day. We were well into the first month before I heard someone mention the Skinned Men again. We were out on the playground and Kyle and I were trying to start a fire with two large wood chips. I'd just given myself a splinter when the distant sound of metal grinding on metal flooded onto the playground, silencing every one of us.

"Borrasca," I said in awe.

"Yep," said Phil Saunders. "The Skinned Men kill again."

"Kyle said only little kids believed in Skinned Men." I threw an accusatory look at Kyle.

"They do! Phil is just stupid."

"Screw you! Why don't you ask Danielle, she's seem them." Phil scanned the playground and then yelled at a blonde girl talking to Rude Nose. "Hey, Danielle, come here!"

The blonde girl rolled her eyes but came skipping over anyway. "What do you want? I already told you Kayla doesn't like you, Phillip."

"No, tell them about the Skinned Men." Phil gestured to the air around us which was filled with the metallic scraping coming down from the mountain.

"Why don't *you* tell them."

"Because you saw them and I didn't."

"*I* didn't see them, Paige saw them."

"Oh." Phil said and an uncomfortable silence descended.

"You guys are weird," Danielle said before flipping her hair in our faces and leaving.

"Who's Paige?" I asked when she'd gone.

"Her sister," Phil said.

"Paige disappeared when we were like 5." Kyle said.

"After she saw the Skinned Men," Phil added.

The sounds from the mountain abruptly ended and the subdued atmosphere of the playground disappeared with it. When the bell rang we lined up with our respective classes. Since Phil was in my class, I made sure I was behind him. The teachers began to count us off.

"Hey, what else do you know about Borrasca?" I whispered to him.

"My brother said that's where people go when they disappear. To Borrasca to meet the Shiny Gentleman."

"What happens to them there?"

"Bad things," he said, and then shushed me when I asked him what he meant.

The year dragged on and it wasn't until Christmas break that I heard the machine at Borrasca again. It was December and there was a thick blanket of snow on the ground which only served to amplify the noise from the mountain. I sat in my room listening to it for a few minutes trying to decide what was happening in the place that bad things happen. I saw my dad's cruiser pull up out the window and went down stairs to meet him. As I passed my sister's door I heard her giggling in that annoying, teenage girl way and I cringed. I hoped Kimber never got like that.

"Hi Dad," I said to him as he opened the door. My dad stomped the snow off his boots and smiled up at me.

"Sammy! How many years has it been?" He joked.

It was true I hadn't seen much of my dad lately since he was working so much. Doing what, I didn't know since this was the quietest, lamest town ever. Mom thought the Sheriff was grooming dad for his job since Clery was so old and Dad never really agreed or disagreed with her. He'd only been at the department seven months, after all, and my dad doubted people in the county would vote for him.

"Feels like about six this time!" I laughed. "But, um, do you hear that noise in the distance? That like machine-sounding noise?"

"Yep! I hear it in town every now and then, too."

"Do you know what it is?"

"You know I asked the Sheriff that same question and he told me that noise is coming from private property up in the Ozarks."

"Is the property called Borrasca?" I asked quickly.

"I have no idea. Borrasca? Where'd you hear that?"

I shrugged. "Kids at my school."

"Well, it's nothing to worry about, Sammy, probably just some logging equipment."

"But is the place called Borrasca? Like have you heard that name before?"

"No, I have not heard that name before." Dad pulled his boots off and shrugged off his coat, looking toward the kitchen. I could tell I was losing him.

"Have you ever heard of the Skinned Men?" I asked quickly.

"*Skinned* Men? Good god, Sam. Is your sister telling you these stories?"

"No." But he wasn't listening to me anymore.

"Whitney!" He yelled up the stairs.

"No, Dad, Whitney doesn't even talk to me." I repeated.

I heard a door creak open upstairs and Whitney peered over the railing, phone in hand and an annoyed look on her face

"Are you trying to scare your brother?" Dad demanded.

"Dad, no." I said again.

Whitney shot me a venomous look. "Ugh, seriously? As if I'd waste my time."

"You aren't telling him stories about 'Skinned Men'?"

"No, Dad, I told you I heard it at school," I said.

Whitney gestured to me as if to say 'see?'

"Alright, well you kids really need to start getting along anyway. You're family for Christ's sake." Whitney rolled her eyes and when Dad walked into the kitchen she stuck her tongue out at me.

"Real mature, Whitney!" I yelled up at her but she was already gone. "I'll tell Dad about your boyfriend!"

Christmas came and went with surprising smoothness at our house. Whitney and I got almost everything we'd had on our lists, which was a first for us. The town may be smaller but Dad's paychecks were clearly bigger.

I wore my new Ram's parka on the first day back to school after Christmas break. Kyle fawned over it and Kimber showed off the blue pearl necklace her mom had gotten her for Christmas. Kyle and I feigned interest but did it poorly. Kimber knew, but just seemed happy we cared enough to fake it.

As we said goodbye to Kyle for the morning Kimber was suddenly slammed from the side. Kyle caught her before she fell and I spun around angrily to see Dark-Haired Girl – whose name I'd learned was Phoebe Dranger – laughing and walking away from us with Round-Face.

"You guys are assholes!" Kyle yelled at them. "When I'm your boss someday I'll make you clean bathrooms!"

"Yeah, and if Kyle's your boss, you *know* you messed up." I added. Kyle and I high-fived and turned to Kimber but she wasn't impressed with us – I could tell she was trying to hide her tears in her scarf.

"Don't sweat those girls, Kimber, nobody likes them. People are just nice to them because they're related to the Prescotts." Kyle tried to give her an awkward pat on the back but Kimber turned away from him and ran in the opposite direction.

"I hate those girls. Like I really hate them." I said.

"I know, they're bitches." Kyle agreed.

"Well, I'd better get to class and make sure they don't try and talk to her again."

"There's an assembly this morning. No class until after lunch."

"Seriously? That's awesome! Do we have to sit by class?"

"I don't think so but we'd better get there quick so we can get seats at the back." Kyle said as we started walking.

"What's the assembly for?" I asked.

"It's either D.A.R.E. or the History Society presentation."

"What's D.A.R.E.?"

"You know, D.A.R.E.? As in 'don't you dare do drugs or you're grounded until you're dead'?"

"Oh. I hope it's the history thing then."

We found Kimber already in the auditorium. She had collected herself and saved us both seats at the back of the room. She waved us over just as the puffy, stern Mrs. Tverdy walked onto the stage.

"Everyone please quiet down. This morning we have a special presentation for you from the History Preservation Society of Drisking. If you have questions during the course of the lecture, please raise your hand."

"Like *that'll* happen," Kyle laughed.

"Now, I'd like to introduce to you Mr. Wyatt Dowding, Ms. Kathryn Scanlon and of course, Mr. James Prescott."

"What! Jimmy Prescott and not his dad? That's so weird!" Kimber whispered.

"Dude, Thomas Prescott has done this presentation every year for like 20 years," Kyle said. "It's definitely weird."

"It's not weird," whispered Patrick Sutton from behind us. He leaned forward. "Tom Prescott went crazy like a year ago. He didn't do the presentation last year when my sister was here either."

"I don't like Jimmy Prescott," Kimber shook her head. "He gives me the heebie-jeebies. His dad is so much nicer, he's like a grandpa."

The presentation was as slow and boring as it possibly could be. Mr. Dowding and Ms. Scanlon talked about the first settlers here: the Cherokee and the trail of tears. They talked about Alexander Drisking's discovery of a motherlode of ore in the mountains and settling here with his family to mine and refine the iron. Then James Prescott took the stage from there to tell the story of his family's early journey to the town and their role in the revitalization of Drisking itself in the late 50's.

The Prescott story was the first interesting thing I'd heard all morning and I found Jimmy Prescott to be infallibly charismatic and entertaining. I was so busy laughing at his jokes and absorbing his stories that by the end of the presentation I realized I'd actually learned quite a bit. So much so that I was interested enough to ask a question, which Kyle quickly warned me was social suicide.

Mr. Prescott scanned the room and answered a few other questions before he finally got to me at the back.

"Yes, the young man in the blue shirt."

"Um, Mr. Prescott, why did the mines close? Are there any still working?" I asked.

"That's a very good question. What did you say your name was?"

"Um...Sam. Walker."

"Ah, I believe I met your father the other day at the Sheriff's office. Welcome to Drisking! As for your questions, most of the mines were closed in 1951 after a long period of unprofitability: the mountain had simply ran out of iron ore. The mills and refineries were abandoned and the town suffered for years. The miners and their families moved away, stores went out of business, schools closed and Drisking became a ghost town, as I was explaining before.

That would have been the end of it if it weren't for stubborn families like mine who refused to leave. We refused to give up the town and after many, many years of hard work Drisking became the picturesque little haven in the Ozarks that it is today. As for your second question, yes, I believe there may still be one mine in operation. Good questions. Anyone else?"

I sat back down and Kyle shook his head at me. "Bro..."

The assembly suffered through another fifteen minutes of awkward Q and A until Mrs. Tverdy finally cut us loose. We were released into the cafeteria to wait for the lunch lines to open. Kyle, Kimber and I sat in our usual corner.

"That was SO boring," Kyle whined. "When are they going to realize that *no one* cares about Drisking's history? Seriously, I fell asleep like three times."

Kimber nudged me. "Sam seemed to care," she teased.

"I just wanted to know about the mines. Mines are creepy, that's all."

"Yeah, but all our mines were blown up. You can't go in them anymore." Kyle said.

"Blown up?" I asked.

Kimber nodded. "Some kids died after going into the mines so the city set off some 'controlled blasts to implode the caverns', at least that's what my mom said. They messed up, though, and I heard they blew up the water table or poisoned it or something."

"What, how do you know that?" Kyle asked.

Kimber shrugged. "I heard my dad talking about it."

"Did they use C4 or something?"

"I guess."

"So like, we all drink the water so we all have C4 in our bodies and we could explode at any minute!" Kyle said excitedly.

"Do you think that's what happened to all the missing people?" I asked him. "Just sitting there one day and BOOM!"

"Yeah, dude," Kyle grabbed my shoulders. "And that's where the Skinned Men come from."

I made the popular gesture of 'mind blown' and we laughed hysterically.

"You guys are dumb," Kimber rolled her eyes but then she laughed when Kyle fell on the floor pretending he was exploding. I remember thinking in that moment that I was happy here in Drisking, Missouri with these two people. Happier than I'd ever been anywhere else.

It was the last truly moment of joy I ever had. Less than an hour later Mr. Diamond's phone rang and he exchanged a few quiet words with the person on the other end, his eyes flicking to and from my desk. It was hard to be surprised, then, when he hung up and asked me to come up to the front.

He quietly told me that my mom was waiting for me in the office and I was going home for the day. I traded a confused and worried look with Kimber and then packed up my backpack and went to the office. When I got there, my mom was crying.

We drove home in a strained silence. I was too afraid to ask what was wrong. Mom stopped the car a block from our house, which was blocked in by several police cars. When an explanation wasn't forthcoming I broke the silence myself.

"Is it dad?" I asked quietly.

"No, honey, Dad is fine," she whispered.

"Then what is it?"

"Whitney- Whitney never made it to school this morning." Her voice broke over my sister's name.

"Oh." I said. "Oh! Wait, I think she ditched, Mom! I actually saw her leave this morning and it was really early, like 6, and she was with her friends. Um, Pete Whitiger and that kid Taylor!"

"We know about all that, Sam. But they made it to school and Whitney wasn't with them. They said she wanted to stop by the Circle K near Drisking High so they left her there. And no one has seen her since."

"Well..." My brain struggled to come up with an explanation. "Maybe she's ditching."

"No, honey." My mom put the car back in drive and drove up to our house, parking behind a police cruiser. "The police, as well as your father, think that Whitney is with Jay."

"But she has a new boyfriend here!"

"We found all her books on the floor of her room this morning and half her clothes gone along with some cash of your dad's."

"But-"

"Right now we think that she hitched a ride to St. Louis and that she's with Jay. The Sheriff's office is trying to contact the boy's parents now."

Whitney? Run away? Anyone who knew my sister knew she was prone to dramatics and empty threats. Plus, she was dating Chris Whitiger's older brother Pete. I was sure of it.

We walked up the steps and into a house of stale coffee and quiet murmurs. I tried to remember if Whitney herself had ever actually confirmed she was dating Pete but I drew a blank. When we walked into the kitchen, I saw my father sitting at the table staring at phone records, head in hand. He looked up when I came into the room and gave me a weak smile.

"Hey, buddy."

"Dad, I have to tell you something."

I felt a heavy hand on my shoulder and turned to look up at a solemn Sheriff Clery.

"Everything and anything you might know, son. No matter how trivial you think it is."

I nodded and sat down at the table with my dad as my mom handed the big man a cup of coffee.

"Here you go, Sheriff," she said, weakly.

"Please, Mrs. Walker, call me Killian."

My mother nodded and retreated back into a darkened corner to talk quietly with Sheriff Clery's wife, Grace.

"What do you know, Sam?" My dad asked as he rested his chin on his interlaced hands.

"Well, just, I heard Whitney had a boyfriend, that guy Pete Whitiger that she's been hanging out with, and I saw them and Taylor Dranger leave this morning before me."

"What time did they leave?" Asked the Sheriff.

"I don't know...like before seven."

He nodded. "That matches the statements of Taylor Dranger and the Whitiger boy." My father's head sunk lower into his hands and I knew I'd let him down.

"But," I rushed, "I don't think she went back to St. Louis because she was dating Pete and I don't think she wanted to be with her boyfriend back home anymore."

"I understand that, Sam, but a teenage girl's mind is a complicated thing. My officers are trying to get ahold of the boyfriend's family back in St. Louis." Clery nodded to my father. "Now why don't you head up to your room and let us work, Samuel."

I looked up at him in surprise. "What? No I wanna stay down here and help."

"No, son, there's nothing more you can do here. You've been a good brother, now let us handle this."

"But I can help!"

"You already have."

"Dad!" I looked over at my dad with begging eyes.

"Go to your room, Sam." He said quietly after a moment. I balked.

"Dad..."

"Now."

I was so angry. I turned away from them in a rage and stomped upstairs, slammed the door behind me when I got to my room. I sat down on my bed in disbelief. The tears came then and I laid down feeling helpless, worthless and scared for my sister.

I thought about all the places Whitney could be. Was she scared? Was she alone? Was she...dead? When the sun began to set, I finally got out of bed and went to check my email. I was expecting lots of messages from Kimber and Kyle but there was only one.

Did Whitney go to the treehouse?

I sat staring at the computer screen for a long minute, Kimber's words from last fall tumbling around in my brain.

"If you enter the treehouse without the proper ceremony you'll disappear and then you'll die."

I didn't buy that Whitney had gone to Circle K that morning and I especially didn't believe that she'd hitchhiked out of town. Nothing they were saying downstairs made any sense if you knew my sister – but maybe this did. Maybe she and her boyfriend went to the treehouse to make out or something and maybe he'd left her there. Maybe she'd gotten lost or maybe the Skinned Men had found her. That was the worst thought of all.

I didn't need to sneak out because the police were too busy with my parents to care about me anyway. I snuck my bike out of the garage and rode the three miles to the West Rim Prescott Ore Trail. When I got there I was surprised and relieved to see two bikes already locked to the signpost and my two best friends sitting in the snow next to them.

"I knew you'd come," Kyle said when I pulled up to them and Kimber jumped up to hug me.

"I'm so sorry, Sam."

There was really nothing for me to say and they didn't push. Kimber took my arm and we started up the trail. The silence between us was stretched, but comfortable. We trudged through the snow and all the while I searched for the telltale shoeprints of Whitney's wretched Ugg boots but the snow was coming too fast to see. The hike up the mountain was harder and wetter than when we'd come in the fall and when Ambercot Fort finally came into view over the ridge it was a welcome sight. The sun was getting low and we hadn't brought flashlights.

I stumbled as I ran up to the tree, calling my sister's name in the quiet wild. Kyle was right behind me and leapt impressively onto the rope ladder, climbing quickly up the planks. I kept calling Whitney's name, waiting for Kyle to yell that he'd found her or some sign of her.

And then Kimber quietly said my name from where she stood at the Triple Tree. I ran over and followed her finger to what I already knew was there. I found it, freshly carved near the top.

Whitney W.

My breath froze in my chest and my vision blurred with unwelcome tears. And as the sun took its last desperate breath before plunging into the deep of the horizon, a deafening metallic whirl rang out from the wilderness and spilled down the mountainside.

BORRASCA
PART 2

Underneath the Triple Tree there is a man who waits for me and should I go or should I stay my fate's the same either way.

"Good morning."

The words faded back into the ether and I awoke with a start. Jimmy Prescott was lounging against the wall near the door, an amused yet slightly disapproving look on his face.

"Shit, sorry Mr. Prescott. I didn't hear you come in."

"You know I worked here when I was a kid, too, Sam. I installed the bell on the front door for this very reason. Didn't seem to wake *you* up, though," he laughed. I mumbled another apology and idly straightened a stack of business cards in front of me.

"Late night?"

"Ah...kinda." *Very.*

"I hope you weren't out at the bonfires with all the other underage drinkers."

"No, sir." *Of fucking course.*

"Good. Anyway, I'm just here for my lunch. I'll take a parmesan chicken with avocado on rye."

"Yes, sir." Happy that the conversation was over, I walked over to the sandwich counter and unwound the twisty tie from the rye bread.

Jimmy Prescott stepped back from the counter and idly studied the pictures on the wall, though I knew he'd seen them a thousand times before. Most of the photos were of the Prescott family, taken over the last half. I'd always though it odd décor but then the shop did belong to the Prescott's after all.

"Is Meera here?" Prescott asked as I wrapped up his sandwich.

"She's in the back."

"Ah, I thought she'd still be in St. Louis. Well, when you're finished would you mind getting her for me?"

Shit.

"Yes, sir."

I handed him his sandwich and went to the back to find my boss. She was in the office, furiously punching keys on her accounting calculator.

"Uh, Meera? Jimmy Prescott is out front. He wants to talk to you."

She turned and gave me a dubious look. "Did he say what about?" I shook my head.

"Okay," she sighed. "You can go home for the day, Sam."

"Oh...are you sure?" I still had three hours on the clock.

"He's the only customer we've had since we opened. Don't worry, I'll pay you for a whole day, kiddo."

"Thanks, Meera. Um, good luck I guess."

I gave her a sympathetic shrug and she patted my arm. I don't know how she did it. Meera was perhaps the most burdened and stressed out woman in all of Drisking but she never failed to be unbelievably kind. There was a hopelessness about her, a sadness that she hid very well.

I left the store out the backdoor so I wouldn't have to see Jimmy Prescott again. His weird, yellowed amber eyes always set me on edge. Not to mention he was a total tool.

I hopped in my car and texted Kyle that I was off work. He answered immediately and told me where to meet him. I happily whipped my apron off over my head and threw the car into reverse. Crystal Lake was my favorite place in all of Drisking.

I had to park almost a mile away since the lake was so packed. I eventually found Kyle and Kimber sitting on a rock that jutted out over the beach.

Kimber was sunbathing in a blue, floral bikini and Kyle was wearing his 'you can't tell where my eyes are looking' sunglasses.

"What'd I miss?" I asked, sitting down next to Kimber.

"Not much," she answered, stretching and sitting up. "Just more beer." She dug into the cooler behind her and tried to hand me a Blue Moon.

"Ugh, no." I waved it away. "Got any Excedrin?"

"Oh no," Kimber gave me her pitying pout.

"Okay, then I'll just take those sunglasses." I held my hand out to Kyle who looked back at it in horror.

"What? No, fuck off!"

"Oh, come on, Kyle, give him your sunglasses. Sam didn't get to sleep off his hangover like we did!"

I smiled at Kyle and he tightened his lips. We both knew exactly what I was doing. Kimber stroked Kyle's arm in encouragement. "Please?" she asked.

"Fine," he said and shoved his BluBlockers at me. I put them on and sat back, turning my head to watch the girls on the beach below. Phoebe Dranger – the Dark-Haired girl - was there lying on a towel next to Round Face and giggling. It still seemed unnatural to me to see the two of them without Rude-Nose. Those three had been inseparable for years, working as fluidly together as the gears in a watch until Kristy had fallen in love with some college kid and run away.

"So why'd you get out of work early anyway?" Kyle asked.

"Prescott came in."

"Eww," Kimber squirmed. "He totally freaks me out. He's been staring at me since like 7th grade."

"Next time he stares at you let me know and I'll knock him the fuck out." Kyle had always been protective over Kimber but ever since they'd started dating he'd gotten 10 times more unbearable.

Kimber winked at him. "So what did he want, Sam?"

"He wanted to talk to Meera. Probably about the shop."

"You mean about how no one goes there and the business should have closed years ago but it won't because the Prescott's are stubborn and vain?" Kyle said.

"Yeah, probably, I mean she looked pretty worried. I can literally count on one hand how many sandwiches I've sold in the past month. "

"Ouch." Kimber grimaced.

"Yeah. I'm pretty sure she's going to get chewed out. I really don't like that guy." I thought about the squirmy, yellow-eyed freak yelling at the sweet, kind-hearted Meera and it made my blood boil.

"You should have met his dad," Kyle snorted. "He was a piece of work."

"His dad?"

"Yeah, Tom Prescott.," Kimber said. "The family put him in a home a few towns over."

"Really? Why is he in a home?" I asked.

"I heard that he got dementia and he was embarrassing the family in public." Kyle said.

"I heard that, too," Kimber brushed her long curls off of her shoulders. "I always liked Tom Prescott. It was a pretty shitty thing to do."

"Hey kids!" We turned in unison so see Phil Saunders come stomping out of the bushes behind us with Patrick Sutton following behind. "So this is where the cool people hang out. High above the kingdom on Pride Rock."

"Sup Patrick," Kyle said ignoring Phil, whom he'd disliked ever since Phil had briefly dated Kimber. Phil was either unaware of or uninterested in Kyle's feelings. Of course, it may also have been because Phil was stoned out of his mind most of the time, and today was no exception.

They sat down next to us and Patrick offered me his pipe. "Wanna hit this?"

I did want to hit it, and pretty badly too. I reached up to grab it but Phil swatted my hand away.

"Careful, guy, you don't want to get the Sheriff's son high. For fucks sake, Patrick." Patrick nodded knowingly and shoved the pipe back into his pocket.

I scowled. "Really?"

"Sorry, Sammy. Hell, the only reason I'm even smoking *around* you is because today is my cousin's Deathiversary and I don't give a shit about anything else."

"Your cousin Hannah?" Kimber asked with a sympathetic look.

"Yep. 5 years she's been gone."

"Too many people disappear in these woods, man," Patrick said as he exhaled a cloud of smoke.

"Yeah, man," Phil nodded. "You know sometimes, when I'm high, I can see them all. And I feel like I know the answer to the mystery, man. Like I'm so close to solving it. It's just something I can see. Like they're all puzzle pieces and in my mind I see the puzzle put together but I can't tell what the picture is of, you know?"

"You're fuckin' high, Saunders." Kyle said.

"We all are, man. We all are. Everyone in this town is drinking the fuckin' Kool aid."

Kimber raised an eyebrow at him but said nothing.

"Everyone except the dead ones. I can see what they looked like before they went into the ground. Or is it the grounder?"

"Shit's fucked up, Phil." Patrick said to the space in front of him.

"Yeah. I see all those people. Hannah. Paige. Jason Metley. Hell, I ever see your sister, Walker."

Kyle, who I knew had been monitoring the conversation for any mention of Whitney, sprang to his feet and opened his mouth to yell at Phil.

"Nah, the Walker girl ran away to St. Louis, remember?" Patrick said before he could.

I saw Kyle and Kimber exchange a quick look as I tried to remain impassive from behind the BluBlockers.

"That true, man?" Phil asked. And there it was.

I knew Kyle and Kimber had always wondered what I thought about Whitney and if I'd ever accepted the official statement that she and Jay had run away together. They were kind enough not bring it up but I knew they wanted to know what I believed, what I thought had really happened.

I loved them both and I wanted to talk to them about it but I just couldn't. Everyone thought that I had spent the last five years quietly grieving and that I'd put the pain behind me. At least, that's what I'd tried to show them had happened.

The truth was that I'd never given up on Whitney. I'd waited years for Jay to show up on social media and when I finally found him last year, I'd been devastated. I'd always hoped the official report was true and that Whitney was somewhere far away from here, alive and happy with Jay Bower. But his Facebook page showed a thriving college kid, still on good terms with his parents, his ex-girlfriend Whitney the furthest thing from his mind.

When I'd brought the evidence to my dad he'd read the pages I'd printed off and then shut the door to his office with me on the other side. I heard him crying in there for hours as I waited for word that he'd reopened the case and was bringing the smack down to the Butler County sheriff's department. But he'd emerged hours later, his face dry and all business. Justice had never come and we never mentioned Jay Bower again.

For whatever reason, I never told Kyle and Kimber about the incident. Maybe it was because I was worried they'd blow it off like my dad had or maybe, far more likely, I didn't want them to know how obsessed I'd become with Borrasca and the Skinned Men. I knew, as assuredly as the sun would rise tomorrow, that Whitney's death had happened there; just like all the others who'd gone to the Triple Tree.

I was suddenly very aware of 4 pairs of eyes staring at me.

"Yeah, it's true. She ran off with this guy Jay from our hometown." I answered. That was enough for Kyle.

"Alright, guys, seriously, he's the sheriff's kid. What do you think's gonna happen if he gets caught with weed?"

"The little man is right, Phil, let's bounce. I don't need any more trouble with the cops around here." Patrick said.

"Later, Walker. Kimber. Little man." Phil stood up, brushed off his pants, and jumped from the boulder onto the sandy beach below. He sprayed sand all over a couple of freshmen girls who squealed and called him an asshole. Phil tipped an invisible hat to them. "Ladies." He said before walking off.

Patrick followed him off the rock and as I watched them make their way down the beach I became aware of the conversation going on behind me.

"I didn't say I *wanted* to go, I said I *had* to go." Kimber said.

"But it's only 2 o'clock and it's Sunday."

"I know but my parents have been fighting a lot lately and I don't want to leave my mom alone too long."

"I thought she was doing better?"

"A little, but she's still depressed, Kyle."

"Do you wanna stay over at my place tonight?"

Kimber's voice dropped into a whisper. "I just don't…I don't think I'm ready for that yet, Kyle."

"No, wait, that's not what I meant. I'd sleep on the pullout in the basement and you would have my room." Very awkward silence. "My parents love you, you know," he added.

Kimber laughed. "I know. I just want to be there for my mom right now. But thank you, sweetie." And then the absolutely disgusting sound of my best friends kissing. I would never get used to it.

"Ugh, on that note, I'm outta here, too." I stood up and gave them both a shaming look.

"Oh, come on Sam, don't be jealous, we'll find you a girlfriend someday," Kyle joked.

"I really don't need your help with that," I muttered, glancing down the beach to where Emmaline Addler was sunbathing. "I'll see you guys tomorrow."

"Last week of school!" Kimber yelled at my retreating back. *Thank god.*

Tomorrow was the last Monday of the school year and while I should have been thankful my sophomore year was ending, I wasn't. The summer meant no distractions, more time to think and even more hours of boredom at Prescott Artisan Sandwiches.

But I wasn't looking forward to tomorrow for another reason: besides it being Monday it was also Sophomore Ditch Day. My dad had caught on to that several weeks ago and warned me to "set a good example" and go to school that day. Sometimes I really hated being the son of the county sheriff.

Kimber and Kyle were sympathetic and had offered to share in my misery. I had, of course, said yes, much to Kyle's sadness.

As I'd expected my dad was waiting for me when I got home. We shared a brief, strained conversation about our respective days and then he finally got to it.

"Remember, Sammy, we're cracking down on truancy this year. I want to see you at school tomorrow."

"Yeah, I got it Dad."

"And I hope I won't see Kyle's name cross my desk, either."

I sighed. "It's just a tradition, even the teachers sort of encourage it. On Friday they said-"

"I don't care what they said, Sam; besides the fact that I'm the sheriff, I'm also your father and I want my son in school."

I laughed and shook my head. What a joke. "I can't control what Kyle does."

"Fair enough but you *can* control what you do."

I said nothing and Dad sighed.

"It's almost over, Sam. Just get through these last five days and you can be done with school for a few years if that's what you want."

"Fine." I walked out of the kitchen effectively ending the conversation. I climbed the stairs and passed by Whitney's door on the way to my room. The light was on and silence was behind it. I knew my mother was in there. She was always in there, doing god knows what.

I walked to my own room, shut the door behind me and locked it.

The next day at school ended up being more embarrassing than anything else. There were a few other people that hadn't skipped, maybe a total of eight of us, and the looks they shot at me made it clear that my dad was the reason they were there.

Kimber, great friend that she was, happily went to her classes like it was a normal day. Kyle attended all of my classes with me. The teachers, who had been looking forward to an easy day, couldn't have cared less.

Just before lunch an officer came around to all the class rooms and asked for copies of the attendance sheets. Dad really wasn't kidding about cracking down this year. I was going to get shit from people all summer.

At lunch Kyle and I went out to my car to smoke. Usually we were hidden by dozens of large pick-up trucks but today we were out in the open and vulnerable. I moved the car back to a shady corner of the parking lot and Kyle pulled out his bowl.

"Did you text Kimber?" I asked him while he hit it.

"Yep," he said through tight lips as he let the smoke sit in his lungs and then blew it out all over my dashboard. "She went home around 4th period. She said her mom called her and she was going home to take care of her. I don't know, man."

"Doesn't her mom hate you?" I asked, taking my turn with the bowl.

"Yeah. I mean that's a fairly new development, ever since Kimber and I started dating. But I'm pretty sure she's always hated me and just hid it better before. Now that she's all depressed and whatever she doesn't give a shit."

It was hard to picture anyone hating Kyle. "Why can't Kimber's dad take care of her?"

"I don't know."

I hit the pipe again.

"Hey man, let's not even go back today." Kyle said.

"You think?" I asked.

"Yeah, I mean you put in 4 periods, you've been a good son. And Officer Dick Ass already came around and collected the attendance sheets."

"Dick Ass? Really? You're better than that, man."

"Officer....Ass...Dick?"

"You're fuckin' baked, Kyle."

"Seriously, man, let's go."

I thought about it a second. Kyle was right, I'd done my duty as a son and if I left now I'd have enough time to go to GameStop before work.

"Fuck it." I turned the key in the ignition.

Kyle sat up in his chair and rolled down the window to clear out the smoke. "Hey man, can you drop me by Kimber's?"

"Sure but how're you gonna get home?"

"Can you come get me after work?"

"What if her mom throws you out again?"

Kyle rolled his eyes. "That was one time."

"Why can't I just drop you at home and you can take your own car?"

"It needs new tires."

New tires, of course. What Kyle really meant was that his insurance had lapsed and he didn't have any money for gas. He'd bought the car last summer after working double shifts at the convenience store for half a year. It was an okay car, newer, but I knew he'd only wanted it to impress Kimber, something he'd vehemently denied. Had it worked? I really didn't think so.

They'd started dating in the fall and Kyle had quit his job to spend more time with her. Kimber didn't seem like the kind of girl to be impressed by a Pontiac Bonneville but Kyle was convinced that was how he'd won her over. I was sure all the car had really done was give him the confidence to ask her out. And now that its part in their romance had ended, the car sat in the garage of the Landy home collecting dust instead of memories.

GameStop didn't have what I wanted and neither did Prescott Games and Media. Since I had nothing else to do I decided to show up to work early and hope that Meera would cut me loose early, too.

I parked in front and walked in the door, unsurprised to see no one at the front counter. Only three people worked at the shop and sadly I never got to see the other girl, Emmaline, who worked on the days I didn't. This was especially disappointing to me since she was half the reason I'd applied there in the first place.

I went into the back to tell Meera I was there and found her slumped over her desk on a pile of receipts and paperwork. This wasn't an unusual way to find Meera but something seemed different today. I immediately felt a disturbance in the force but before I could quietly retreat she turned toward me and I saw what I had only sensed before - Meera was crying.

"Are you, um....um, are you-"

"I'm sorry, I'm sorry," she said quickly, wiping her eyes. "Is it four already?"

"No, it's 2:15. I just thought maybe if I came in early-"

"Oh right, it's your ditch day." Meera wiped her eyes only to have them fill with tears again. "I don't understand, Sam, this store, this store has been operating in the red ever since I was hired to manage it. What am I doing wrong?"

"I don't...know," I offered lamely, the instinct to escape never stronger.

"No one comes in here – ever - and Mr. Prescott refuses to let me put signs up to advertise! He says they're unsightly, but how does he expect me to pull in business? I need this job, Sam, god, I just..."

I must have looked like a frightened deer because when Meera finally looked up at me she seemed to subtly collect herself. "Go ahead and go out to the front. I'll do your timecard."

She didn't have to tell me twice. I really liked Meera and I hated seeing her like this.

The front didn't end up being much better. I could hear Meera crying over the store's dated music track. Her sobs went from painfully audible to muffled whimpers. After half an hour I decided I had to do something. Since I was entirely unequipped to deal with an adult woman's emotional breakdown I decided to call Meera's husband Owen. He was thankfully at home and answered on the second ring. "I'll be right there."

I breathed a sigh of relief when I heard a truck pull up outside and saw the tall, yet girthy Owen step out of it. He walked in during a quiet lull in his wife's sobs.

"I'm sorry to call you at home, Mr. Daley, I just didn't know what else to do..."

"That's okay, Sam, you did the right thing." He looked tired, as if this situation wasn't new to him.

"Is she ok?" I asked.

"Oh...yeah." He nodded. "We're just going through some things."

"Oh yeah. Meera said the store is going bankrupt." I winced as soon as the words were out of my mouth.

"Yeah," Owen ran a hand through his hair. "That's part of it, although I don't think Jim is going to let that happen. Meera is more upset about..." he sighed. "Has Meera told you about her, ah, appointments?"

"Ah...no."

"Well, the thing is we've been trying to have a baby for years. Very long, painful years. It's just so goddamn important for her to have a baby. And you know she blames *me* for our fertility issues?"

He walked around the room, glancing at the pictures on the wall and not really talking to me anymore.

"I understand why it's important to her, I just don't understand the *obsession* with it, you know? Because she's the last one in her family? Because she's the last McCaskey on the planet? I mean, does she even realize that our baby wouldn't *be* a McCaskey? He'd be a Daley! I tell you Sam, never marry a woman with a crazy father and four dead uncles. They develop these obsessions with lineage and-"

"Four dead uncles?"

"What? Oh, yeah. The famous ones. You know the four brothers who died in the Drisking mines? Well that only left her dad. And her parents were only able to conceive her. Which leaves her as the last McCaskey and 'hope for the family line'. So of course you see how this is all *my* fault."

I looked at him blankly and he sighed.

"I'm sorry, kid. These aren't your problems and they're way over your paygrade anyway. I'm just very stressed out right now. Our medical issues and Meera's absolute abhorrence to our only other option, I just-"

"But how did they die?" I was desperate to talk about anything else and the story of Meera's uncles interested me.

"The McCaskey boys? I don't really know. They died on the mountain somewhere."

"Oh. Well, um, have you heard of the Skinned Men?"

"Skinned men?"

"Yeah."

"I don't think so."

"What about Borrasca?"

Owen Daley squeezed his eyes shut and pushed in on his temples with his fingers. "What? What does a borrasca have to do with anything?"

"Owen?" Meera voice squeaked from the doorway.

"Oh, baby, are you okay? Sam called the house-"

"I want to do it."

"You do?" Owen asked dubiously.

"I called him."

His eyes flicked over to me and I immediately looked away. Another conversation I didn't want a part in.

"Sam, why don't you take off for the day? Meera and I will handle things here."

"Okay," I mumbled and bolted for the door. Once I was in my car and backing away, I called Kyle.

"Dude, fucking weird shit is going on in this town."

"What happened?"

"I can't explain it over the phone. Where are you at?"

"I'm at Kimber's. Are you off work?"

"Yeah."

"Can you come get me?"

By 'at Kimber's' Kyle meant sitting on the curb in front of the house, kicked off the property again. When I pulled up Kimber came out and met us at the curb.

"I'm so sorry, Kyle," she said. "She's really upset today, she wouldn't even let me leave the house to sit with you."

"It's okay," he said. "Don't worry about me I just want to make sure you and your mom are okay."

"We're okay. And my dad will be home soon."

"Text us when he gets home and we'll come get you." I said.

"I wish I could, I'm babysitting tonight until 7:30. Maybe after that?"

"Sure."

Kyle and Kimber hugged goodbye and then Kimber rushed back to her house as something crashed inside.

"So what's going on?" Kyle asked, taking a sip of a warm Dr. Pepper sitting in my cup holder. "You're still wearing your apron, you know."

"Meera had a breakdown," I said, peeling it off.

"Really? What happened?"

I told Kyle the full story paying particular attention to the four uncles.

"Yeah the McCaskeys. I've heard of them. Didn't know Meera was one, though, I thought they were all dead."

"Yeah, she's the last one. So like...do you think the McCaskey deaths have anything to do with the *other* disappearances?" It had been awhile since I'd mentioned anything about Borrasca and Kyle choked a little on the warm soda.

"I don't...I don't know, man. I mean maybe if the disappearances started around the same time?"

"How can we find that out?"

"Maybe the cops? There have to be police reports."

"Okay, but what if I couldn't ask my dad?"

Kyle shook his head. "I don't know then."

"What about like records? The historical society people, maybe?"

"Oh yeah," he said, nodding. "We can try them. They're over on 2nd. They share an office with Drisking Arts and Antiques."

I made a U-turn and started back toward town.

"Hey, ah, Sammy...why are we doing this?"

I'd known the question was coming but I'd hoped to have more answers myself before giving him one.

"It's just...Whitney," was all I could say. Kyle didn't ask anything more. The History Preservation Society of Drisking was at the back of the Antiquities shop and the owner - a wan, stone-faced Mr. Dranger - eyed us warily as we walked through. At the end of a short hallway we found a small room with two desks pushed together. One was empty and the other was stacked high with books and folders of loose paper. We could hear someone typing behind the stacks.

I cleared my throat. "Hello?" A small woman popped up from behind the desk. I recognized her as the same woman who had given the us the lecture in 6th grade. "Hello. How can I help you boys?" She asked, walking out to greet us.

"Um, yeah, I have a few questions about Drisking's...history, I guess?"

"Oh great! Is this for an end of year report? Have a seat, boys." She gestured to the empty chair sitting behind the other desk. I nodded at Kyle and he sat down, looking uneasy.

"Yeah, it's for an essay we have to write. Hey, I think you gave a lecture to us like five years ago with Jimmy Prescott."

"Oh yes! I give that lecture every year with Mr. Prescott," she smiled.

"Yeah it was you and one other guy, too. A bald guy." Kyle said, shifting uncomfortably in the wooden chair.

"Yes, that was my fiancé Wyatt Dowding. He passed several years ago."

"Oh." Kyle said.

"So, ah, Miss- Miss-"

"Scanlon. But you can call me Kathryn." She said.

"Kathryn," I tried. I hated calling adults by their first names. "Um, we want to know about the McCaskey kids."

"Ooh," Kathryn said shaking her head. "A dark part of history there but history nonetheless."

"Yeah, so when did that happen?"

"And how did they die?" Kyle added.

"Well they didn't die. I mean, they certainly perished in the mines but their bodies were never recovered so we don't know the answer to that. I would think dehydration, starvation and exhaustion killed them within days of getting lost down there. And to your second question that was...1953, I believe."

"And the mines closed that year?"

"Well actually the mines officially closed the year after. There was a legal spat between the city and the Prescott family who wanted to leave the mines open until the bodies were recovered. But the city won and the mines were condemned."

"Wait, why did the Prescott's care?"

"Don't you want to write this down?" Kathryn asked.

Kyle tapped his temple twice with his finger. Kathryn shrugged and continued.

"Well, the Prescott and the McCaskey families were closely related. Tom Prescott was paying teams of unemployed miners to go down in the mines and search for the bodies. The city had had enough of it, the mountain was unstable and they didn't want any more deaths. The mines had been abandoned years before and were structurally unsafe. After the city banned the Recovery teams from the mines, members of the Prescott family started going down there themselves. One of them, a cousin I think, died during the search

156

from a fall down a shaft and the city had finally had enough. Less than a week later they hastily had the mines collapsed."

"With bombs?" Kyle asked.

"Well, with explosives. And that's what led to the 'incident' as it's called. By this time the mines had been unprofitable for a few years and the city was quite broke. They hired a less than reputable company to collapse the mines and, well, when they set off the explosives, they accidentally broke into Drisking's water table. The city went into debt trying to purify the water of silt and iron ore. It wasn't until two years later that things started getting better, thanks to the Prescott's who truly did revitalize Drisking."

Kyle's phone chirped and he pulled it out of his pocket. "It's Kimber. She wants us to come over."

"Okay. Thanks Ms. Scanlon. I mean, Kathryn"

"Sure! If you have any other questions feel free to come by. We're almost always open during the day. Oh! Or you can email me." She dug into her jacket pocket and pulled out a loose business card. It was creased and had a dusty smudge on it.

"Thanks."

"So what do you think?" Kyle asked when we got to the car.

"I don't know. It's weird isn't it? I mean why would the Prescott's give a shit if the town suffers after they refused to help them find their family and were actively working against them?"

"Maybe they forgave and forgot." Kyle shrugged.

"Does Jimmy Prescott seem like a guy to forgive and forget to you?"

"Ugh...no. And his dad is even worse."

"Exactly. Maybe we should-"

"Turn here! Sorry, Kimber's still babysitting and she's over on Amhurst." When we pulled up Kimber was out in the driveway with two young boys who were playing in the front yard. She was holding a sleeping baby and waving to us. We parked in the driveway and she introduced us to the two older kids. They gave us shy hellos and then ran off to continue their game.

Once they'd left we explained everything that had happened that afternoon to Kimber while she listened and rocked the baby in her arms.

"Well, Sam is right, that doesn't make sense. But why are we even concerned about something that happened decades ago?"

"Whitney." Kyle said so I didn't have to. A flash of surprise crossed Kimber's face and she walked over to put the baby down in his playpen. Then she walked back and pulled me into one of her famous Super-Comforting-Not-At-All-Awkward Kimber hugs. When she released me she began to pace around the driveway. "Okay, so we think Whitney somehow got involved in all of this and, you're right, if we want to figure this out we need to start at the beginning. Phil is right: every mystery in this town is one piece of a larger puzzle, it's all related..." She stopped and looked over at us. "I think we need to go to the source if we want answers."

"Yeah that's not a bad idea," Kyle agreed. "I know he likes to hang out in the Hide-away and get drunk with ex-Sheriff Clery."

"Ah, no Kyle. Not Jimmy – his dad."

"Tom? No way! He's so crazy they put him in a home!"

"He's the horse's mouth, though, isn't he? Jimmy isn't likely to know half as much as his dad."

"But-"

As Kyle and Kimber argued I watched the kids chase each other around the tree in their front yard. There seemed to be something carved in the bark, words, not unlike the Triple Tree at Ambercot Fort. I was too far away to read what it said.

"He got you, he got you!" I heard the youngest one call to his brother. "The Skinned Man got you, now you have to die."

"Na-uh, Peter, I was touching the tree."

"No you weren't! You're a liar! One of them got you and now you have to meet the Shiny Gentleman!"

"No I don't!"

"Kimber, Josh is cheating!"

I shuddered and turned away from them. "Where's the nut house?" I interrupted them. "Is it close?"

"It's not a *nut* house, it's more like a hospice," Kimber chided. "The rumor I've heard is that he's at Golden Elm and that's in Cape Girardeau."

"That's about 40 minutes away," Kyle said and pulled out his phone. "I'll check the visiting hours for Tuesdays. Sam, do you work tomorrow?"

"I work every day but I'll get out of it." I promised.

"Ok cool. Let's plan to leave after school."

The following day dragged on like any last Tuesday of the school year. Most people talked about what they did with their ditch day or complained about a cop showing up at their house to issue them a ticket while sliding less than pleased looks my way.

When the final bell rang at 3:30 I grabbed my bag and booked it out to my car. Kyle and Kimber were already waiting for me.

The drive took longer than expected when I got lost in Cape Girardeau. The town was bigger than Drisking and the streets weren't laid out with any sort of planning or logic that I could see. By the time we arrived at Golden Elm there were only 20 minutes left for visiting hours.

"We're here to see Mr. Thomas Prescott," Kimber told the nurse at the front desk. We tended to let her do the talking since she had a disarming, old-fashioned charm about her that usually put people in an agreeable mood.

"Old Tom? Wow, he hasn't had a visitor since his son came in around Christmas. You're family then? You know where his room is?" The nurse arched a thin, suspicious eyebrow.

"I'm sorry, we don't." Kimber apologized. "My mother has been asking me to check in on my great uncle while she's away doing Doctors without Borders. I should have gotten more information from her but you know, she only has so many minutes to call home."

"Oh, of course dear! Go ahead and sign in and I'll get someone to escort you."

An orderly led us to Tom Prescott's room which we found empty. He pointed down the long corridor and said "He likes to read in the sunroom."

We walked down the hall and found an old, thin man all alone and whispering to himself. He was sitting at a table sliding chess pieces over a backgammon board.

"Tom Prescott?" Kimber said, smiling.

He didn't look up and I wondered if he'd heard her at all. Kimber took a deep breath to try again but the old man suddenly slammed his fist on the table.

"I'm him, goddammit, I'm Mr. Thomas Prescott. Don't call me Tom; people's kids used to have more respect, you know."

"I'm sorry, sir." Kimber said gently as she sat down in the chair opposite him.

"You kids have no respect. Do you even know who I am? It's my son's fault. That boy's momma shoulda whipped him but she was soft and now he's runnin' around my town spreading his vulgarity and disrespect." He spat the last word out as if it were a salmon bone.

"Our apologies, Mr. Prescott, we never meant to be disrespectful. We greatly admire you. We're from Drisking - you're the man who built our town! Everyone remembers that. Everyone was suffering and the town was dying and then you fixed it. We know that."

"I did what I had to do," the old man grunted. "It was *my* town. It still is. Who are you, little girl, to come in here and suggest otherwise?"

"Ah, no, no that's not what I said." Kimber changed tactics. "And as for who we are, we're Meera McCaskey's kids. Do you remember the McCaskeys?"

"Huh. So you're Aida's granddaughter. That explains why you're not there." Kyle and I exchanged puzzled looks.

"We're right here, Mr. Prescott." Kimber said.

"You know what I meant, young lady! They all know. They know I rescued the town, that's *my* town. Of course they were going to let me do anything I wanted as long as the money kept coming in. That's *why* it's my town."

"Is the money still coming in?" Kimber tested.

"Well, you're here aren't you? They didn't like it but they took the money. They didn't know. Not everything, they didn't, but they suspected some. And they kept electing Clery and they kept taking the money."

Prescott picked up a pawn and ran his fingers over it as he talked. "It's just a powder, you know, so unassuming. A fine, soft powder. The powder doesn't know what it is, it doesn't know it's bad. It's the people who say it's bad. But it needed to be done. You know that, Aida, you know we had to do it." Kimber hooked him in. "I know. I know we had to it but it's your son. I don't think he's doing it *right* anymore."

"Well of course he isn't!" The elderly Prescott slammed his fist on the table again and two rooks tumbled to the floor. "They were mine! He took them from me. He thought he could do it better but he took mine and he ruined my legacy. Decades of work and now it's all run by the powder. The dust of my crumbled empire!"

"What about the Skinned Men?" I asked, caught up in the moment.

"What are you talking about, boy?" He growled.

"And the treehouse! The Triple Tree, what is it? What is it for?"

"Triple Tree? Is that what he's offering again? We paid triple the price but it was only for a short while, when things were slow. We certainly never *charged* triple, that's just bad business."

"Where is Bor-"

"Has my idiot boy been telling you that? Did he offer you triple for them? He's ruining my town, isn't he? Goddamn it, Jimmy, you get him in here! Aida, get my boy on the phone, you tell Jimmy I wanna talk him! You tell him they're still mine! Aida! Aida, get Jimmy on the phone!"

Kimber jumped up and Kyle pushed her behind him as the old man rose to his feet, tall and surprisingly imposing for his fragility. We were already backing toward the door when the orderly came in with a disapproving look on his face and shooed us out. Long after we'd made it to the lobby we could still hear Tom Prescott yelling for his son.

The ride home was quiet and I spent it trying to fit the pieces of the puzzle together. The Skinned Men, the Triple Tree, the Shiny Gentleman, the powder. These things seemed to have been pulled blindly from the ether, random and meaningless. The veil over my eyes was thick and heavy but I was closer to Borrasca than I'd ever been before. I could feel it all around me, I just couldn't *see* it.

I snapped out of my thought when I realized Kyle was pulling over off the road. He put the car in park and turned around to look at me in the backseat.

"Is this really about Whitney, Sam?"

"Yes."

Kimber watched us with worried eyes.

"Why? The cops, I mean, even your father confirmed that Whitney ran away."

"I don't believe them." I said through clenched teeth.

"Look, Sam, we're getting pretty deep in here and I am with you every step but I have to know that there's a reason we're doing this.

161

And pulling Kimber in, too. I have to know this is important to you for the right reasons and not just an…obsession."

I looked out the window and realized he'd pulled over near the West Rim Prescott Ore Trailhead. He was right to worry and even more so to be protective of Kimber. Kyle was thinking it and so was I: it was all about the powder. If Borrasca really did involve moving drugs did I want to involve my friends any further? This wasn't their fight. I loved these people, could I really risk their safety for my own curiosities and vendettas? But as hard as I wished I could let them go I knew I needed them in this with me.

"I have to know what really happened to Whitney." I said quietly.

Kyle turned back around without a word and Kimber placed her hand on mine. I jerked it away and crossed my arms but immediately apologized. Kimber just smiled in a forgiving sort of way.

Kyle sighed. "Sam…"

He was interrupted by the piercing ring of Kimber's phone. She scrambled for her cell to silence it but when she saw the name on the screen she quickly answered.

"Dad?"

.....

"What? Wait, what- what do you mean?"

.....

"Dad, hello?"

......

"No, wait, slow down. Hello?" She took the phone away from her ear. "Something happened to my mom and she's at the hospital." She said in a sort of shock.

Kyle threw the car in gear and screeched out of the parking lot. We made the 10 mile trip to the hospital in as many minutes, which was criminally fast on surface streets. Kyle slammed on the brakes at the emergency entrance and Kimber and I ran inside.

A deputy was already there waiting. He refused to answer Kimber's desperate questions as he led us down the hall to her father. When the deputy swung the doors open I saw my dad standing next to Kimber's and I immediately braced myself for the worst.

Kimber's dad took her in one direction and my dad and I went in another. Before he said a word to me I saw Kimber crumble to the floor on the other side of the room. I looked at my dad for confirmation and he gave me a sympathetic nod and pulled me into a hug.

We sat down in a corner and I stared at my hands as he quietly explained that Mrs. Destaro had gone grocery shopping at around 1 o'clock, come home, put the groceries away, made two lasagnas and a meatloaf and put them in the freezer. Then she got in her car, drove to the hospital, parked in the shade, took the stairs up seven floors to the roof and jumped off of it. She lived long enough to apologize to the EMT who found her.

I watched Kimber wail from across the room as her mother's body grew cold in the morgue beneath us.

*

"Do you think she blames herself?"

"I don't know, man. Probably." I stretched out on the reclined seat of my Chevy and pulled the bill of my hat lower over my eyes.

"But do you think she's okay?"

I didn't answer him. I certainly hadn't been okay when Whitney died and Kimber was even closer to her mom than I was to my sister. She was definitely not okay. "Sam, seriously. I'm fucking freaking out here, it's been two days."

I pushed my hat up off of my face and looked over at Kyle who was admittedly a wreck. His eyes were bloodshot, his face sallow and his red hair was slick with grease.

"Dude, her mom committed suicide. You how close Kimber was to her mom. She just needs some time but she'll be okay."

"She hasn't answered any of my texts or calls. I've left her like nine voicemails, man, I think *I'm* going crazy."

"You just have to give her space."

"Yeah, but she's my- my-..." He still couldn't say it around me. "I'm supposed to be looking after her."

I sat up and pulled the chair upright behind me. "Look, Kyle, I know you want to help Kimber - I want to help Kimber too, but she hasn't answered our calls, been to school or come to the door when we've gone to her house. She doesn't want to see us. Right now Kimber knows what's best for Kimber."

"What about the suicide note? You think that has something to do with it?"

I sighed. "We don't even know if there *was* a note. Kimber's dad was pretty messed up when he said that and I probably misheard him, anyway. I asked my dad and he said there was no letter."

"Right, because your dad is such a beacon of truth." One look at Kyle told me he immediately regretted his words. I shrugged.

"I don't know what to believe anymore."

The truth was that I was sure of what I'd heard. Mr. Destaro *had* said something to the cops about a letter, but I couldn't tell Kyle that, not right now. He was already worried that his relationship with Kimber was part of the reason her mom had been so depressed.

I'd asked my dad about the letter when he'd come home after that long night and he'd sighed, run both of his hands through his hair in a tired sort of way and said, "Sam, I don't know what to tell you. Anne Destaro didn't leave a suicide note and this is the first I've heard of it."

With our best friend in mourning and our investigation on hold, Kyle and I had been existing in a sort of suspended state. We went to school intermittently, skipping classes here and there, missing end-of-year tests and smoking more weed than either of us could afford. Without Kimber there to set us straight and keep us in line we were lethargic, brooding, and irresponsible. I'd never realized how much I relied on her.

Kyle and I skipped the last two periods of the day and debated on whether we should even go to school the following day, which was the last day of our senior year and graduation. We finally decided to show up for second period, which was fortunate because Kimber showed up in Biology.

I didn't even see her at first. I had my head down on my desk resting on my folded arms when I felt a meek hand pat my shoulder. I turned around to see her standing there, looking unsure and uncomfortable. I gave her half a smile and pulled her into a hug. But it wasn't a Super-Comforting-Not-At-All-Awkward Kimber hug. It was a longer, weaker hug and I felt so protective in it that I was sad when it was over.

"How are you doing, K?" I asked her.

Kimber wiped a tear off of her cheek. "I'm okay." She gave me a wobbly smile and I knew it wasn't true.

I wrapped her into another quick hug as Phoebe Dranger gave us a snotty look. "Have you seen Kyle yet?"

"No. I have next period with him."

"He's been worried about you."

"I know," she said, sliding her eyes to the floor. "Things have been...really hard for me at home."

"It's okay," I said, "we're here for whatever you need."

"Yeah, that's...that's what I was hoping."

"Whatever you need."

Since it was the last day of school our teacher, Mr. Founder, was just happy to return our graded tests and let us bullshit for the rest of the period. Kimber talked about the arrangements for the funeral that weekend and chided me for skipping finals to get stoned. When the bell finally rang I could tell that Kimber was both excited and nervous to see Kyle. As we packed up our bags I assured her that Kyle wasn't mad, he was really just worried about her. She threw her bag over her shoulder, set her jaw and nodded. Kimber was trying so hard to keep it together.

As soon as Kyle saw her from down the hall he slammed his locker shut and walked towards us with such intensity that I began to wonder if maybe he *was* mad. He pushed past a dozen people without so much as glancing at them and left a curious, if annoyed, crowd in his wake. When he finally reached us Kyle threw his backpack against the wall and swooped Kimber up in the sort of way you'd see in old, black and white movies. Everyone who'd watched all this unfold, including me, groaned in unison.

Since most of the teachers weren't even bothering to take attendance that day I went to Calculus with Kimber and Kyle where they had the same conversation that Kimber and I had had last period. Towards the end of the hour the conversation faulted and became uneasy. Kyle and I exchanged a look over the top of Kimber's head and I nodded at him.

"Kimber," he said quietly, "did you mom leave a letter?"

"What?" Kimber asked in surprise.

"I heard your dad talking about a letter on the day that- on, ah...on Tuesday." I said.

"Oh."

As we waited for her to continue the bell rang for lunch. Everyone filed out of the room but the three of us, who stayed sitting on our desks.

"Kimber." I finally said.

She sighed sadly and looked over at Kyle. "Yes."

"There *was* a letter? What did it say?" He asked nervously.

"I don't know, I haven't seen it. I asked my dad for it when we got home and he said I'd misheard him and there was no letter. He said not to mention it to anyone else or I'd just upset people."

"Well, then we both misheard him," I said. "Which seems unlikely."

"I've known my dad all my life. And I know when he's lying."

People started to filter in for the next period, sliding sympathetic glances at Kimber. Since it was our lunch hour we gathered up our things and walked out to my car, as we always did. I sat in the backseat, letting Kyle and Kimber take the front.

Kimber took a deep breath and continued. "I know my dad is lying and I know he has the letter."

"Are you sure?" Kyle asked. I could tell he was still terrified that some of the blame rested on him.

"Yeah. And all I know it contains the name 'Prescott'."

"*Prescott?*" Yet somehow I wasn't surprised. He was the axis around which everything bad that happened spun.

"How do you know it says Prescott?" Kyle asked.

"I heard my dad reading it once. I think he reads it a lot, actually. He was sort of sobbing and whispering the words and throwing things in his bedroom. My dad...he hasn't been well."

"Do you think she was having an affair with Jimmy Prescott?"

I shook my head. "I'm guessing you need to think bigger than that, Kyle."

"I agree," Kimber said to her lap. "With everything we know about the Prescott's I'm fairly sure this isn't about an affair. It's all connected somehow, don't you think? My dad was the love of my mom's life but she only left a letter for me. I think that somehow I'm the one she wronged, not him. You know? I think she did something to me. Or...maybe she did it because of me." Kimber's voice broke over the last sentence and Kyle pulled her over, kissed the top of her head and whispered words to her that I couldn't hear.

"So we need to get the letter," I said after giving them a minute.

"Yes. I really need to read it." Kimber's voice was still wobbly.

"How do we get it?" I asked.

"If it's in his bedroom we just need to wait until her dad isn't home." Kyle said as he looked out the window.

"You don't think I thought of that?" Kimber sighed. "He never leaves his room, not since we got home from the hospital. He *sleeps* in there."

"So we need to get him out."

"No, we need to get *me* in. Tomorrow is my mom's funeral and half of Drisking will be there, including my dad of course. I need to leave without him noticing and run home so I can go through the office."

"Okay, that's easy," I said.

"Without my dad noticing. And I need to be back by the end of the service."

We both nodded but stayed silent because it looked like Kimber was weighing saying more.

"My dad...he's been very cold and I think...I think he blames me." Kimber finally said.

"That's bullshit." Kyle spat.

"Can you guys help me?"

"Absolutely."

"Of course."

We spent the rest of the lunch hour creating a plan far more strategic than the mission probably called for. Kyle and I would engage Mr. Destaro in conversation and then Kyle would get a "text" from Kimber telling him she was having a breakdown in the bathroom. Kyle would leave to go "comfort" her and they would take my car to the Destaro house. I would stay behind and keep an eye on Kimber's dad while they were gone. We all decided that in light of everything that was going on, we would skip graduation that evening.

I went to work in the afternoon for the first time since Monday. Meera seemed to be in a much better mood and let me go home early for the graduation ceremony that I wouldn't be attending. I went straight to bed, skipping all my parent's concerns about the milestone I was missing out on by deciding not to walk that evening. I didn't sleep well. Just before 4 a.m. I got up to go through my clothes looking for something dressy and black to wear to the funeral.

My dad came in before he left for work and found his disheveled, panicked son looking helplessly through piles of black and gray clothing. He smiled sadly and led me to his own closet. Since my dad and I had not only the same face but the same build as well finding something suitable to wear was easy. I thanked him and he asked me to apologize to Kimber for having to work through the service and that he sends his love.

Anne Destaro's funeral was at an Episcopalian church on the other side of town. I picked Kyle up at 9 and saw he was also wearing a suit of his Dad's though he didn't fit it nearly as well and he was constantly pulling at the sleeves and readjusting the waistline. Unfortunately for Kyle he was much taller than his dad.

We parked as far away from the church as possible in a spot no one would notice a car leaving from.

When we went inside the church we saw that Kimber wouldn't have to do much acting to convince people she was having a breakdown. She was at the back of the room, tucked into a chair, just a puddle of curly red hair and tears.

Kyle sat down next to her and pulled her into a hug. "Jesus, Kimber, what's wrong?"

I kicked his foot and shot him a look that said 'really?'. Kyle bit his lip. "I mean, ah... Fuck."

"There's no one here," Kimber whispered against his chest "My mom grew up here, she had hundreds of friends in this town and no one came!"

We looked around and I had to admit, the turnout was sparse. A few groups of three or four people standing together, Kimber's dad who sat in a chair opposite the room of his daughter and some family I recognized from BBQs at Kimber's house. Ex-Sheriff Clery with his wife Grace were there, standing with a few of my dad's deputies and talking quietly in the corner. I could see why Kimber was upset.

As we waited for the service to start I realized with a profound sadness that I'd never been to a funeral before. I wished that we'd had one for my sister but I knew we never could since Whitney was still legally alive. It made my heart break to think that she would never be laid to rest.

Only a few other funeral-goers trickled in and the Pastor began getting people seated for the service. I noticed the casket at the pulpit for the first time and was glad it was closed. Still, I had to wonder at the simple, unadorned, almost ugly coffin that had been chosen for Kimber's mom. I knew the Destaros had money, quite a lot of it, actually. It was an interesting, almost insulting choice. My heart went out to Kimber.

As a somber music began to fill the room Kyle and I stood Kimber up and started over to the pews. Halfway there, she stopped. "I'm ready," she said and brushed the hair away from her wet face.

"Ready for…?"

"To leave. I can't be here anymore, it's a disgrace to my mother." Kimber raised her head a notch and squared her jaw. I knew this look - there would be no reasoning with her.

Kyle and I looked warily at each other. It would be a lot more obvious that Kimber was missing from the service with the low turnout.

"You guys go over and say what we rehearsed to my dad. Kyle, I will text you in 30 seconds. Go."

Kyle nodded and started over and I knew we weren't arguing. Mr. Destaro was finally standing, looking over at the front pew reserved for him and his daughter with an almost nervous hesitation.

"Mr. Destaro?" I said as we approached. "I'm, ah, I'm- I'm very sorry to hear about your wife. She was…" Shit, I'd forgotten my lines.

"-a great woman who raised a wonderful daughter." Kyle finished.

"Yeah?" He spat. "Do great women commit suicide leaving their wonderful daughters behind?"

"Ah…" *Shit.*

"Do great women jump off buildings and make spectacles of themselves? Do they leave their families to deal with the publicity and the grief they caused?"

Kyle's phone chirped. *Thank god.*

"Oh, that's Kimber," Kyle said a little too fast, before he'd had time to actually look at his phone. "Oh man, she isn't well. Says she's crying and feeling sick. I'm gonna go sit with her."

"No!" Mr. Destaro yelled so suddenly that Kyle dropped his phone on the ground, sounding a loud clatter on the stone flooring. "Not you. You don't help my daughter, you don't even talk to her. He can go." And he pointed at me.

"Ah…okay." I stuttered. The plan had changed too much. I needed to somehow get the car keys from Kyle without being seen. Kyle gave me a shaky, subtle nod and then he and Mr. Destaro went to sit down. It was obvious Kimber's dad was keeping an eye on Kyle when he pulled him into his pew at the front of the church. Getting the car keys from Kyle was going to be nearly impossible.

I backed into the shadows at the back of the room while the pastor started the service. I texted Kyle four times asking for help but he wouldn't dare touch his phone. He just stared straight ahead, flicking worried glances at Mr. Destaro every few seconds. After several minutes I went to find Kimber to see what she wanted to do but she wasn't in our meeting place by the back door. The plan was falling apart.

I pulled out my phone and sent her a text.

Me: *Where are you?*
Me: *Kyle is next to your dad and I can't get the keys from him.*

I waited in the hallway, tapping my phone against my hand nervously. After a minute or two my phone vibrated.

Kimber: *Kyle slipped me the keys. I'm sorry, I left without you guys. I had to get out of there. I'm so sorry, I'll be back before the end of the service, I promise.*

Shit.

Me: *Be safe.*

It was now imperative that I not be seen. I went to the men's bathroom, locked myself in a stall and played Brick Breaker for the longest twenty minutes of my life. I knew the service wouldn't go on much longer so I texted Kimber again.

Me: *You on your way back, yet? Did you find it?*

I sat waiting, watching the minutes tick by. I texted her again.

Me: *I think the service is ending soon. Where are you?*

After another seven minutes of no response I tried calling but it went to voicemail. I tried again with the same result. I was getting nervous. I was about to try a third time when a texted popped up from Kyle – the service was over.

Kyle: *Why aren't you guys back yet? Did you find anything?*

I left the bathroom stall and found Kyle staring out the window looking for my car.

"Kyle."

He jumped. "Where's Kimber? What did you guys find?"

"I don't know, she left without me."

"What the fuck, why? Where is she?"

"I don't know, Kyle, she left *without* me." I reiterated. "She's not answering my calls or my texts."

"Fuck, mine either."

"We have to keep an eye on her dad until she gets back."

"We're not the only ones," Kyle said gesturing across the room. "What the fuck is going on?"

Three men were talking to Kimber's dad in a corner across the room. The tallest was Killian Clery, who was flanked by two of his former deputies. Drisking's retired sheriff had his hand on Mr. Destaro's arm and was speaking to him in an angry, hushed tone. Kimber's dad was shaking his head and desperately objecting to something. The two deputies walked out the front door of the church and Mr. Destaro sagged against Killian Clery who sat him in a nearby chair. Something was happening.

"Call Kimber. Now." Kyle said. I tried again and this time the call rang once and was sent to voicemail. I ended the call and threw up my hands, looking desperately at Kyle.

"Again." He said and took out his own phone. I got the same result but felt relief wash over me when someone answered Kyle's call. My heart sank when I realized it wasn't Kimber.

"Phil, what part of town are you in? I need a ride. It's an emergency."

.....

"Yeah, man, I'm at North Ridge Church. As fast as you can. I'm with Sam. I'll owe you."

Kyle hung up and then immediately tried Kimber's phone. "She's sending me to voicemail, too."

We both stood at the window anxiously waiting to see Phil's silver Mazda pull up. Kyle chewed his lip and I tapped my phone nervously against my leg. *Come on, Saunders.* We threw occasional looks back at Kimber's dad until Clery stood him up and ushered the now inconsolable man out of the church.

Suddenly Kyle's phone chirped and we both looked down to see Kimber's name flash on the screen. Kyle's knees nearly buckled in relief and he sagged against the wall.

Kimber: *I found it.*

Kyle opened the text and furiously typed a reply.

Kyle: *they're coming for you, K*

We both stared at the phone waiting for a response. And just as Phil's silver sedan pulled lazily into the parking lot, we got one.

Kimber: *They're here.*

It was the last message we got from Kimber. When Phil dropped us at the Destaro house we found the front door unlocked and no home. My car was sitting in the driveway, unlocked with the keys sitting on the front seat.

Kyle and I drove back to the church but the funeral was over and the few people that had attended it were already gone. We drove back to Kimber's house again but it was just as we'd left it and still no one was home. Kyle had lost it by this time and was an absolute wreck. He'd called her so many times, I was sure he'd killed her battery. His calls went straight to voicemail and his texts remained unanswered.

After an half an hour of undignified begging from Kyle, I finally called my dad. He answered immediately.

"Sammy? What's wrong?"

"It's Kimber. She's gone, Dad. We've looked everywhere but she and her dad are missing. She left the funeral early and- and- Killian Clery was talking to her dad and then Sampson and Grigg left and I think they went to her house and they got her. I think they're still working for Clery on the side or something and I think they took her somewhere. She-"

"Whoa, whoa, slow down! Come by the station and let's talk. I'll take a statement from you boys and I'll send a couple officers over to investigate the house right now. Just calm down, Sam, we'll handle this."

I hung up and threw my car violently into reverse, jerking the wheel to the left as I hit the end of the driveway.

"Sam. Sam, how do we know? How do we know we can trust the cops?"

"Because we don't have a choice right now. And we're not trusting the cops, we're trusting my dad." I said, my words sounding hopeless, even to me.

I turned into the Butler County Sheriff's office and Kyle was out of the car as soon as I slowed down to park. By the time I got inside, my dad had Kyle by the shoulders and was nodding solemnly at everything Kyle was telling him. When my dad saw me, he motioned for an officer to take us to his office. After a few minutes he came in and sat down across the desk from us.

"Alright boys, I'm going to have Officer Ramirez come in in a few minutes and take an official statement from you both. I want you to know that right now it looks like the Destaros left town voluntarily."

"No, no way, Mr. Walker, Kimber would never-"

My dad held up his hand for silence. "Let me rephrase: Jacob Destaro left town voluntarily. Kimber is a minor and has no legal rights here. If her dad decides that they're leaving, then they're leaving."

"But she's not answering her phone and we went to that house, Dad, nothing was packed."

"Maybe they're just getting away for a while, maybe going to a relative's. I can't theorize as to why she wouldn't answer her phone, other than maybe she wants to be left alone for a while."

Kyle was exasperated. "But-"

"Look, I know it's hard for you to understand but losing a family member takes a toll on a person, Sam you know that. We don't know how people are going to grieve and we don't have a right to. I think it's very likely that Kimber will be back by the fall."

"The fall?! Sheriff Walker, that's three months away, you need to investigate NOW."

"Kyle, I know you're upset and no one said we're not going to investigate thoroughly."

"Like you investigated Whitney's disappearance *thoroughly*?" I spat and I didn't regret the words.

"Sam!" he snapped with more force than I'd ever heard him use. "I am tired of listening to you insulate that I didn't do everything I could to find Whitney. I love your sister more than you can imagine, she's my *daughter*, Sammy. And I will *never* give her up."

"And what about the deputies that left the funeral to go after Kimber?" Kyle interrupted. My dad raised an eyebrow at me.

"Sampson and Grigg, I told you." I ground out through clenched teeth.

He sighed. "Boys, Sampson and Grigg left the funeral because I sent them out on a call."

I stood up violently, knocking over my chair in the process. "Oh come on, Dad!"

"Alright, that's enough!" The sheriff slammed his hands on the desk and stood up. "I told you I would tell you what I know and I have. I understand your friend is important to you and goddamn it, I care about the Destaros, too. I promise you that I will use the full extent of my resources to track them down and put your minds at ease but until then all I can offer you is the assurance that there is no sign of foul play *at this time.* You boys need to get off the warpath and let us handle this. Now Ramirez is waiting in the hall to take your statements and then both of you are going home. Understood?"

I said nothing and glared at my dad, seething with rage. Kyle stood up and walked out of the room with no emotion whatsoever. He walked past Ramirez and I followed him out to the car. We got in and I waited for Kyle to say something. I heard a loud sniffle and looked over at him to see his face slick with tears. It was the first time I'd ever seen Kyle. But not the last.

"He's lying." He whispered.

I just shook my head. I didn't know what to believe.

Kyle turned his face away from me. "I know he's lying. Something bad has happened and he's lying about it."

"Like what?"

I heard more sniffling as Kyle tried to collect himself.

"Dude, fucking talk to me. What do you think happened?"

"Kimber's gone like all the others. She's at the place where bad things happen."

"Borrasca?" I said. And I just couldn't believe it. I punched the steering wheel. How the fuck had this happened? Fuck, not Kimber, please not Kimber. Was all of this because of me? Had her mother killed herself because of something I'd done? Something we'd found out? Was it my fault Kimber was missing? If I thought for one minute that that was true I knew I would crack into a million tiny pieces.

"No. Not Kimber. No."

"Yes, Sam, fucking think about it!" Kyle yelled at me. "It's the treehouse! It's all the same! Borrasca, the Skinned Men, the Triple Tree, your sister, the mountain; it's all the fucking same! It's the Prescott Empire and now Kimber has been fucking- fucking *consumed* by it!"

"Where do we go?" I could feel the warm tears of my own desperation and hopelessness sliding down my cheeks. "What- what do we do? What do we fucking do?!"

Kyle threw his hands up in frustration. "We have to go to Ambercot, right? It all starts and ends at the Triple Tree, Sam. Surely you've figured that out."

"We've been to the treehouse a million times, Kyle, there's nothing there!"

"I don't know where the fuck else to go, Sam!"

RAP RAP RAP

I jumped as someone tapped on the window of the car and wiped the tears off my face. I rolled down the window as Officer Grigg leaned down and looked in the car. "You boys move along home, alright?"

"Yep." I said, and turned the key in the ignition. Officer Grigg waved at us as we pulled out of the parking lot but we didn't wave back.

"The treehouse." Kyle said.

We drove in silence, both of us trying desperately to get ahold of ourselves. If we were going to be of any help to Kimber we needed to be calm enough to think logically. I parked in the space next to the trailhead and saw several bikes tied to the post. As we made our way up the West Rim Prescott Ore Trail we passed Parker coming down it with a couple of his friends.

I nodded to him but Kyle said nothing, just stared up the trail reaching for the only place he knew to go. It was almost dark by the time we reached Ambercot and there was little light left to search for whatever Kyle hoped to find. It took half an hour in the darkness before I finally convinced Kyle that there was nothing there to help Kimber. And the same dense, heavy, black hole consumed my stomach as it had all those years ago when we were here searching for Whitney. This time had to be different.

And though we didn't speak of it, I knew that he and I were both painfully aware of all the sounds of the night. We were scared-chilled down to our very bones - that we would hear the piercing scraping, grinding metal screams of the monster at Borrasca that we'd become so accustomed to over the years. I knew we both dreaded it and prayed it would not come tonight.

I dropped Kyle at home an hour later and promised we would find Kimber tomorrow. I swore we would. He gave me nothing more than a shallow nod and disappeared inside his house. My dad was waiting for me in our kitchen when I walked in a few minutes later. I didn't look at him and walked over to the fridge, realizing I hadn't eaten all day.

"Sammy. Sit down, I want to apologize for today."

I took out some chicken and cheese and went to the pantry for bread.

"I know you're scared. And I know that a lot has been going on that you can't exactly relate to." He sighed. "Anne...Anne had been depressed for a good long while, Sam, over twenty years. That'll weigh on a person."

I ignored him and continued making my sandwich. I was dying inside, wondering if I could even trust the man I'd called Dad my entire life.

"She was suffering, Sam, and sometimes people who suffer that deeply don't know of any other way out. She knew her depression was hurting her husband...and her daughter. And maybe she mistakenly thought she was doing them a service."

"Mom's depressed." I said without taking my eyes from the cutting board.

He sighed. "Your mom is coping okay and this was very different, Sam. Kimber's mother has been depressed since she was in her 20's. Early in her marriage Anne suffered multiple miscarriages. Infertility can be very hard on some couples and not even Kimber's birth could totally ease her pain."

"Fine. I'm tired and I'm going to bed. Kyle and I are getting up early to look for Kimber." I threw the knife in the sink with a loud clang and turned to look at my dad for the first time. "Please tell me you're still trying to find her."

The sheriff stood up from the kitchen table, looking as tired and disheveled as I felt. "I promise, Sammy." And I finally believed him.

The next morning when I pulled up to Kyle's house, Parker came out to meet me.

"Hey, Parker." I said when I rolled down the window and cool morning air wafted in.

"Kyle's not here. He left around 5. Stole my dad's truck. He's pissed so you'd better go."

"Thanks, man." I said, and then rolled up the window and took off down the street. I drove around all morning looking for Kyle and calling his cell but he didn't pick up until around noon.

"Sorry, man. I couldn't sleep." Kyle sounded a bit more stable than yesterday.

"That's cool, where you at?"

"I don't know, exactly. A rare spot where I'm getting service."

"You in the woods?"

"Yeah. She's out here, Sam, somewhere in these mountains. I can feel it. I know it."

"Alright, well let me meet you."

"Ok. Just come down to the West Rim Trail and I'll meet you there."

I was only five minutes away so I arrived before Kyle had time to get down the mountain. Mr. Landy's red Dodge Ram was parked haphazardly in a no parking zone and I figured it would probably be towed by the time we got back. I very much doubted Kyle cared at this point.

I crossed my arms and leaned against my car as I waited for him, staring up the familiar dirt trail that now looked so foreign to me. When Kyle finally showed half an hour later, he was covered in sweat and dirt and dejection.

"So?" I said, pushing up off the car.

"No, nothing, man."

"Alright, well let's keep searching."

We hiked miles and miles of the mountain that day but we didn't find any sign of human life. And for the next few days if the sun was out, so were we. Kyle was growing more and more desperate: crossing onto private property to look for logging equipment and mapping out the county's many mines to search the abandoned buildings. But the mountain was big and the needle buried deep in the haystack. And as the days slipped away so did Kyle's sanity.

Every time I saw my dad he would give me a sober look and promise me that they were still working on Kimber's case. It seemed to me that even *he* was growing concerned. The Destaro house remained as empty and dark as the space between the stars above it.

Eleven nights after Kimber's disappearance I was awoken by the piercing, whirling, screeching sound of death at Borrasca. I cried myself to back to sleep to the tortured din of Kyle's own agony next door. We had failed her. Kimber was dead.

*

When I pulled up to his house the next morning, I could tell it was all over for Kyle. His skin had taken on a yellowed color and his voice was flat and void of emotion.

"It's not over yet, Kyle," I said as he dropped into the seat next to me.

"Yes, it is, Sam."

"No, I don't believe that. Kimber's dad is missing too, you know. Maybe it was him instead that was, that..." I couldn't bring myself to say anything more.

"You know we're living in hell. Drisking, it's Hell in our reality."

I couldn't disagree. The town I'd grown to love seemed so unfamiliar to me now. Whitney hadn't been an outlier like I'd thought, missing people were the norm here. "And that would make Jimmy Prescott the king. He's Satan, himself."

As soon as the words were out of my mouth Kyle punched the car door, awaking from his deadened state with rageful vigor. "I'll fucking kill Jimmy Prescott! Where is that motherfucker? You know he's involved in all this, Sam, you know-"

"Maybe. Partially." I said, staring out the window. "His dad created the town that bred this shit but I'm pretty sure the Prescott's are just running drugs. You know, the powder."

"Yeah... and so what, he's recruiting people to be- to be drug mules or something?"

"Probably." I agreed for Kyle's sake, though I didn't really believe it. The sound, the great beast machine of Borrasca gave off the distinct stench of death. And though I knew that physically that was impossible, to smell death all over the mountain, it didn't change my mind about it.

We drove over to 4th Street Gourmet Coffee and Bakery and went in to buy our usual provisions of Rockstars and beef jerky. As I paid for the four-pack of cans and meat I saw Meera waiting on coffee at the opposite end of the bar. I could tell that she was in a good mood, something that I hadn't seen much of since I'd started working for her. It was probably a good time to tell her I was calling out of work for my 5th day in a row.

"Hi Meera," I muttered when I approached. "Ah...I can't come in again today. I've got some, some really important-"

"Sam! Oh my gosh, how are you?"

"Um...I'm okay." I stuttered.

"Good!" She said, brightly. "Don't worry about coming in, I'll hold down the fort and I'm sure I can call Emmaline in if I need help. But really, Sam, what have you been up to lately that's so important?"

My mind blanked. Just as I started to stutter out some bullshit about helping my dad, Kyle appeared behind me.

"We're trying to find Borrasca." He said with all the gravitas of a eulogy.

"Ah, yes. Owen told me you'd asked him about that. You know that's just a story, Sam; that legend has been around since I was a kid."

"Yeah, well, we're looking for our missing friend, Kimber. We think maybe she's... there," I trailed off lamely.

"Oh really? I thought I heard the Destaros were staying with relatives in Maine over the summer." Meera shrugged. "Anyway, good luck, boys."

"Thanks." Kyle's voice was sour and I knew his patience was thin.

When we got back into the car we each popped open a can of Rockstar and started chugging. I knew better than to ask Kyle if he wanted to smoke since I was sure he hadn't lit a bowl since Kimber had disappeared. He finished the energy drink in under a minute and crumpled the can in his hand.

"I don't like your boss," he said.

"Meera? Why not?"

"I don't know. She's just…off."

"Well she's been going through some shit." I wasn't going to elaborate any further.

"Why were you asking her husband about Borrasca anyway?" Kyle asked.

"I don't know. I was just making small talk and I thought he might know. He seemed to know about a lot of other things."

"And did he?"

"Nah." I took a long gulp of the sour drink and slowly brought it down to my lap as I recalled something Owen had said. "Well, actually, yeah. He called it 'a' Borrasca instead of just Borrasca. You know, like it's a thing instead of a place."

Kyle lowered his Rockstar. "And is it?"

"I don't know. *I've* never heard of it. I've googled everything weird about this town but nothing ever came up."

"Did you spell it right?"

"I don't know," I shrugged. "Do *you* know how to spell it?"

"No."

I pulled out my phone.

"No, fuck google." Kyle said. "We need to talk to Kathryn Scanlon again. That's what Kimber would say."

He was right. Kathryn Scanlon may be the most knowledgeable person in town and was probably the right person to ask. I pulled out of 4th Street Coffee and prayed she was at her office this early. When we parked in front of Drisking Arts and Antiques I was disappointed to see that the store was dark. Kyle pointed to a small, cardboard 'OPEN' sign hanging in the corner of the door and I prayed that it was for Kathryn's office.

I was relieved to find the door unlocked and we hurried past all the antiquities and blown glass to the back of the store where we found an open door and Kathryn sitting behind her desk.

"Boys!" She stood up when she saw us. "You're up quite early for summer break. How did the essay do?"

"Eh...great," I said. "Actually we're here for more help."

"Personal interest," Kyle added.

Kathryn raised her eyebrows. "Color me impressed."

I needed to get right down to it. If by some small chance Kimber was still alive then every second counted. "We're here because we want to know if Borrasca is a thing or a place."

Kathryn raised her eyebrow. "I remember that legend as a kid. I'd actually have to tell you I didn't know if it wasn't for Wyatt. He knew so little about so much," she laughed. "A sort of jack of all trades...anyway, he told me an interesting fact once about Borrasca – it's both!"

"What do you mean?" I leaned over her desk.

"Well the term 'borrasca' is just old, outdated lexicon. The word was used by miners to describe an underperforming mine."

"A mine..." I whispered.

Kyle shook his head. "We've been looking at mines."

"So *all* the mines in Butler County are Borrascas?" I asked.

"Well, generally it's only the first mine in the system to run dry that is called a Borrasca."

"Do you know which mine ran dry first? In our mining system?" Kyle asked from where he stood near the door, repeatedly clenching and unclenching his fists.

"Ah, not off the top of my head, no," she laughed. "I can look though, I think I have those records here somewhere." Kathryn walked behind her desk and opened a drawer of loose files. "This is an odd thing to be interested in for boys your age but I guess I should be glad you two are so eager to learn, especially over the summer."

"Yes, ma'am, very eager," said Kyle.

"Is the Borrasca, the first mine that ran out of ore, um, was that by chance the same one those kids disappeared in?"

"The McCaskeys? Oh no, I don't think so. That particular mine was the southwest mine and was very close to town. I think it was one of the last to close, actually. Ah! Here we go. This folder should have that information."

Kathryn spent far too long moving books around on the desk to make room for the stack of papers she had. Kyle and I paced around the room nervously, trying to appear casually interested while the energy drinks started coursing through our systems.

"Here, we go! The first mine to close was the north central mine, which was…yeah, actually one of the first to open."

"But where is it?" Kyle walked over to the desk and braced his arms on it. "Where is that mine?"

"Um…" Kathryn pulled over a different stack of papers and started to fumble through it. After the longest minute of my life she made an 'a-ha!' sound and pulled out a large, yellowed piece of paper that had been folded into a standard A4 size. She unfurled it on the desk and leaned over to read the markings. I could see from where I was standing near the doorway that it was a map and I knew we weren't living this office without it.

"Let's see. That mine was up further on the mountain, a little harder to get to. See?" And she pointed at a small dot on the map that was at least four miles from where we'd been looking.

"Can we take this?" Kyle asked. "We'll bring it back."

"Of course! I'm sure I have copies. Listen, if you boys are going exploring-"

"I'm bringing my dad." I lied.

"Oh! Excellent then, you guys have fun!" She yelled at us as we rushed out of the building. We didn't stop to answer her, 'fun' was far from our minds.

"It's- it's- it's so far from where we've been looking," Kyle stuttered. "We need to go there now. And we need to get a gun."

"A *gun*? Where are we going to get a gun, Kyle?"

"From you dad."

"He's not going to give us a gun, man."

"Fine, then let's scout the place first and then we'll come back with a gun." That didn't seem like a good idea to me either but what choice did we have? After studying the map for several minutes we realized the easiest way to access the mine was still through the West Rim Prescott Ore Trail.

We parked at the trailhead and made the familiar hike down the well-marked trail and then up the beaten path, realizing that we'd have to travel past Ambercot Fort on the way. And I knew in my heart that we were on the right trail. We were walking the same path that so many people before us had on their way to Borrasca. But what had they found there?

We passed the treehouse, which was as silent as the morning. We walked on in the woods, further north than we had ever been before and soon we were flying blind, hiking in the general direction of the dot on the map and hoping we were still on course. Within an hour I began regretting that we'd come without provisions and that we were exceptionally emotional and unprepared.

By noon we had been hiking for four hours and it seemed to me that we were lost. I tempered the welling panic with thoughts of Kimber and Whitney and the answers to the mystery that had absorbed my life for so many years.

Kyle, for his part, said nothing and kept his eyes straight and his mission his priority. And then, just as the sun teetered on the apex of the day, we saw an emptiness through the trees and the hard lines of manmade buildings. Kyle quickened his step and I rushed to keep up.

When we finally broke through the tree line I choked on my own deep breath and stumbled back against a tree as I looked over the quiet encampment. A large, wooden sign post that was almost as long as the entire clearing was still standing near the entrance of the mine. It had to be a century old and though most of the letters had rotted off over the years, from those remaining I could guess that it had once said: DRISKING UNDERGROUND MINE.

What was left, however was: SKIN ND MIN

"The skinned men." I whispered.

"That way," Kyle pointed to the north end of the camp.

We stepped out from the shadows and into the vulnerability of the clearing. There were several large buildings still standing and the boarded up entrance to the ore mine was set back in the mountain.

"We're not getting in there," I whispered.

"Let's try that building," he said, and pointed toward the closest one, which was the largest and at least two stories tall. We counted to three and then ran across the camp to the large wooden doors of the old building. They were cracked open and when we squeezed inside I had no doubts that death was indeed present at Borrasca.

We were standing in what I guessed was a refinery and in the middle of the room was a large silver, conically shaped machine. A conveyer belt fed into it and the room had a sour smell. Even the dirt beneath our feet seemed to have taken on a crimson tint.

"This is the machine. This is where they take them," I said. "People die in here."

"Kimber isn't here. Come on."

I was only too happy to squeeze back out the door of the building and tiptoe around the side. We rounded a corner and almost ran into a recently waxed, shiny, green truck parked against the building.

"This is Jimmy Prescott's truck," I breathed.

"I know whose truck it is." Kyle growled.

We were now on extraordinarily high alert. Kyle dropped to the ground and began to commando crawl around the building. I followed him waiting to hear a shout or a gunshot but there was only the dragging sound of our bodies through the dirt.

As we crawled around to the back of the building, Kyle turned to me and put his finger over his lips, then pointed at a one story brown building that was only a dozen feet away from us. He got into a crouched position and moved as fast as he could across the gap between the two buildings. I did the same.

As soon as I reached the wall next to him Kyle whirled around and put another finger to his lips and then pointed up to a window directly above us.

There were noises coming from inside and even to me, a 17 year old virgin, the sounds of sex were unmistakable. We could hear an animalistic grunting and the tired, objecting groans of an old mattress. Unable to help myself I whispered "What the fuck?" to Kyle but he was already gone, all caution abandoned, running around the side of the building.

I followed him in through the first door we came upon and was hit in the face by an invisible wall of the stench of great suffering. The smell knocked me back, but Kyle kept running. I followed him in, past crates of ramen noodles, MRE's, bottled water and boxes I had no time to read. I crossed another threshold and I was suddenly surrounded by people. So many people. I skidded to a halt and realized I was standing in a sort of dorm. Rows and rows of beds on either side of me with people strapped to them, some of them wearing dirty rags and some wearing nothing at all.

Many seemed to be bloated and I waited for one to call out to me but they all remained silent, some watching me through tired, dead eyes and others turning away their heads away from me. Looking around I realized they were all women and the bloating I

saw seemed to be…pregnancies. Some were confined to their beds
with straps and others were not.

I looked around the room for Kyle and saw him standing a little
further in the long room looking back at me with the same confused,
wild expression I was sure was on my own face. I saw the realization
cross his bewildered features and called out to him but he was already
running again.

I lost him before I'd taken five steps to follow. I figured it was
probably best to just keep running, spread out and look for Kimber. I
didn't see her in this room and I was sure she would have called out
to us if she was.

I looked around for another door and saw one cracked open on
the left behind a row of beds. I stared straight at it as I made my way
there, desperate to avoid the sad, desperate eyes of the women
around me. First we help Kimber, then we help the others. *I will come
back and help you all, I promise. As soon as I find Kimber.*

Without a thought I pushed the door wide open as soon as I'd
reached it and found the source of the noises we'd heard outside the
building.

It was Jimmy, something I'd been expecting to see, but the scene
before me was not. He was hunched over the bed of an almost
unrecognizable, unresponsive Kristy, treating her like an animal. She
watched me through half-opened eyes but she didn't call to me for
help. I thought I saw a tear run down her cheek before she turned
her face away from me to face the wall on the other side. "What the
fuck?" I didn't even realize I'd spoken out loud. I had never seen this
depth of human suffering.

Jimmy's head snapped around to look at me and briefly
registered surprise before he smiled at me in a way that turned my
insides to ice. He didn't stop what he was doing and I wanted
nothing more than to run over and push him off of Kristy but to my
utter shame I couldn't force myself to come any further into the
room.

"Sam! Sam!" Kyle's voice echoed through the building and
immediately cured me of my paralysis. I found myself running back
into the miner's dorm and away from Jimmy Prescott and the long
suffering Kristy.

"Kyle!"

"Back here, hurry, please, I fucking- I found Kimber!"

I followed his voice through the maze of beds and rooms as a cacophony of noise began to follow me.

"Help us. Please." Their voices were weak.

There were maybe only a handful of girls yelling at me but it sounded thunderously loud as if filtered through my guilt. The weight of their misery dropped down upon me and it almost pushed me into the rotting, wooden floor.

"I will! I'll get help, I'll help you!" I promised them as I followed Kyle's voice, still screaming desperately from an adjacent room. I sprinted across another threshold and saw him, hunched down near a corner bed helplessly yanking on a leather strap attached to the post.

I slammed into the bed and fell to my knees, trying to work out what he was doing and how I could help him. I tried not to look at the bed because I knew I couldn't see her like that, I couldn't bear it. If Kimber looked at me through the same accusing, empty eyes as Kristy and the others I might lay down on the ground beneath her and curl up into a ball.

"Go around the other side! Unbuckle the other two straps!" Kyle had the high pitched voice and wild, desperate eyes of madness. I ran around the other side and did as he'd said with shaking hands.

"Oh, boys!" Jimmy's voice rang out from somewhere in the building. I had just freed Kimber's ankle and was working on her wrist. She whimpered when she heard him and buried her face in my shoulder. "Do you think you're hiding? I know where to find you. I know right where I put that girl."

"I'll fucking kill you, Prescott, you sick cunt! I'll fucking stomp all your bones and bleed you out you little motherfucker!" Kyle had lost all reason and strategy. He was filled with rage instead of fear and it scared me even more. I pulled Kimber's wrist from the final strap and yelled, "Go now!"

We pulled Kimber up off the bed and quickly realized that her legs could barely support her. She was heavily sedated and breathing weakly. We braced her on either side and moved as quickly as we could through the nearest doorway – away from Jimmy.

We were in another dorm, though this one was filled with mostly empty beds. I could see sunlight shining through the door at the end of the long room and we raced toward it as Kimber made little cries of pain. I didn't think my heart could break any more but I was wrong because in the next moment it shattered into splinters.

I almost dropped Kimber when I saw her staring at me. Her eyes were hollow and uninvested and when I turned toward her, she looked away immediately as if she couldn't stand the sight of me.

"Whitney." I said weakly.

"Sam, let's fucking go!" Kyle screamed.

"I can't." I turned toward him as tears ran down my hot cheeks and Kyle saw her too.

"I can't...I can't stay," Kyle said, still moving toward the door. "I have to get Kimber away from here. Please..." But he knew I wasn't going anywhere now.

"Good luck, bro." I said and then we were both running in different directions.

Whitney's hair was long but it was thin, as was her face. Everything on her looked brittle except for her stomach which bubbled out from her like an overblown balloon. She refused to look at me and flinched at my touch as I tried desperately to unbuckle her from the bed. I hadn't even finished the first belt when I heard Jimmy walk up behind me. I didn't bother to look at him or stop trying to free my sister. I didn't know what else to do.

"I admire your grit, kid." Jimmy said, and then sat down on a bed behind me and continued to watch, giving no objection to what I was doing. "You probably think your friends will get away but there's no sense in false hope, is there?"

"There's no sense in any of this." My voice sounded frail and it cracked over the last word.

"You're wrong about that," Jimmy sighed. "But just so you know, I've got Clery out there looking for them already. People make a lot of noise coming down off this mountain, trust me on that."

"Sheriff Clery?" I was desperate to keep him talking, anything to keep him from trying to stop me.

"Oh, yeah. You know he was supposed to retire from the business but unlike the previous sheriff he kept a few horses in the race."

"Horses?" Nothing made sense.

"Yep." Jimmy slapped the bed next to him. "We call these buildings the stables," he laughed.

I dropped the last buckle on the floor and looked down at Whitney. I expected her to spring up and run toward the door while I went after Prescott but all she did was rub her wrists and itch her collarbone. Then she put her arms back where they'd been, turned her head away from me and shut her eyes. I slumped down onto the bed next to her and picked up her cold hand. If she wasn't leaving here neither was I. It was over. I sent a silent prayer up to a God I didn't know and wished my friends safety.

"Do you want to know what this is, Sam?"

I shrugged. It didn't seem to matter now.

"You should know, this might all be yours someday. You see, it's all about the babies."

I stared down at Whitney and her swollen belly but gave no indication I was listening.

"You wouldn't believe how much money is in the industry. I mean, my dad was a smart man. And he knew we didn't have anything of value to sell and back then the Prescott's were dirt poor out of work miners just like everyone else in town. He first got the idea when he sold my older brother off to pay for the legal fees to fight the city. I mean, some people will pay five figures for a newborn, you know, even back then. And the organizations that buy them, well, they buy in bulk. But we still make a killing off them. And our overhead is very low as you can see."

Jimmy stood up and pulled a gun out of his waistband, then threw it on a bed across the aisle.

"You know, try to understand, Sammy, it's not just about the money. We use the stables for community services, too. Lots of people in town come to us, you know, ever since the incident in the 50's."

I couldn't take it anymore. I didn't want to be here, listening to this, I didn't want to see Whitney so broken and I didn't want to wait for inevitable death. It was torture in its purest form.

"What are you waiting for, why don't you just kill me? This isn't a James Bond movie, I don't care about any of this shit."

Jimmy laughed loudly as if it was funniest thing he'd ever heard. "Kill you?! Christ, kid, if I could than I already would have, but I'm not allowed to kill you. I've been trying to decide if I want to fuck your sister right in front of you though. She's not one of mine but it might be worth it just to see your face."

"Just- just kill me and let her go. Fuck, I'll kill myself if you let her go." I stood up from the bed and Jimmy took two steps toward me and punched me so hard in the face that I thought I heard my cheekbone crack. I grunted and fell back down on the bed, fighting the stars and tears behind my eyes.

"I can't let her go, you little fuck. She's got one of our community service babies in her. Grace says she's got another week to go, two tops." Jimmy looked down at Whitney and frowned. "She's been puttin' out shit babies, though, and as soon as this one's out of her she's got a date with the Shiny Gentleman."

"What the fuck does that mean?" I yelled at him and a loud ringing suddenly filled the room. Jimmy held up a finger and pulled a phone out of his pocket.

"I gotta take a business call. Two minutes and we can get back to our conversation." Jimmy walked over to a corner of the room and I desperately started to pull on Whitney.

"We gotta go. We gotta go, Whit, we can't stay here." She kept her eyes shut and her body lax. "Whitney, they're going to kill you!"

My head whipped toward the door as I heard a truck skid in the dirt just outside of it. Jimmy ended his phone call and Killian Clery walked in, pushing a limping, bloody Kyle in front of him. "Lose something, Prescott?"

"Where's the girl?"

"Couldn't find her."

"Goddamn it, Clery, you fucked us. Go back out there and find that girl!" Jimmy snatched his gun off the bed and shoved it into the back of his waistband.

"Now listen here, you little shit," Clery growled. "I ain't your fucking employee and I don't have all fucking day to play Hide and Seek in the woods. I'll telling you she wasn't with him so I guess if you wanna know where she is you should get it outta him!" Clery threw Kyle down on the floor and spit near his feet.

"I gotta do *your* fucking job now?" Jimmy walked over and without any hesitation kicked Kyle so hard in the ribs I heard some of them snap inside his chest. I tried to stand up but I was still dizzy and still fighting off the darkness. "Where's your girlfriend, Landy?" Prescott raised his boot and then stomped down hard on Kyle ankle. He screamed in pain. "I can do this all day, kid."

Clery sat down on a bed across the aisle and lit a cigarette, watching impassively. Jimmy pulled Kyle to his feet and then punched him hard in face. A few of Kyle's teeth scattered across the floor. "Tell me, you little cunt!" Jimmy punched him again in the face and Kyle went limp.

"You're killing him!" I screamed and jumped off the bed, running blindly toward Jimmy in a red rage. Clery stood up and caught me with no effort at all, holding my arms down at my sides. He laughed, cigarette still tucked into the corner of his mouth as I struggled helplessly against his chest.

Jimmy had straddled Kyle by now and was rapidly punching him in the face and chest. Kyle was barely conscience and I prayed he'd pass out from the pain. After a full minute of this Jimmy stood up and rubbed his bloodied fists. "Last chance, Landy."

"Fuck you." Kyle said through a wheezing, rattled breath of air. Jimmy spat on him, raised his foot up as high as he could and brought it down on Kyle face with so much force that I heard his skull break. I sagged in Clery's arms and he dropped me into a puddle at his feet.

Jimmy bummed a cigarette off Clery and they stood next to Whitney's bed, watching me cry. "Jesus, what a mess."

After a few minutes Clery flicked his cigarette out and pulled out his phone. "Alright, Sam, take your friend."

I couldn't have heard him right.

"Fuck that, that little Landy shit ain't leaving here."

"You wanna clean this mess up, Prescott?"

I stood up and my knees didn't buckle beneath me. "I'm not leaving without my sister." I told them. Jimmy laughed.

"Yes, you are," Clery said. "If you want to save your friend's life. He ain't dead yet, Sam, but he will be soon." He tossed his keys at me. "The road off this mountain is back by the refinery."

I let the keys bounce off of me and fall to the floor. Clery swore at me. I knew he was right. I was a coward and I would leave my sister and all the others here just so I could get away and save Kyle's life.

I picked up the keys and then, without looking at the two men, I grabbed Kyle by his shoulders and his head rolled back as if it was no longer attached to his spine. His face was a collage of pulp and blood and I struggled to stay calm and breathe as I dragged him out of the building. Clery and Prescott watched me, taking drags off their cigarettes and saying nothing. I knew they were probably lying to me;

Kyle would be dead by the time I got down the mountain if he wasn't already.

I opened the door to Clery's old Ford and pushed Kyle into the passenger seat, wincing as his head rolled around like a ball on a string. It took me almost an hour to get down the mountain, even though I took the overgrown road at ridiculous speeds and did everything I could to destroy the shocks on the truck. I sped into the hospital's emergency zone and found a medical team waiting inside the door. It was clear that they'd gotten a call to expect me because they already had a crash cart with them and an IV ready to push into Kyle's wrist.

I left Clery's truck where it was and spent the next two hours in the waiting room, calling my dad over and over again and crying over an Architectural Digest magazine. No one came to take a statement from me or ask me any questions. Kyle's mom arrived just before my dad and started screaming as soon as she saw me. My dad walked in behind her and had a deputy restrain her. He drove me home in silence but I couldn't take it for long.

"Is anyone going to file a police report? Does anyone even fucking care what happened?"

"Sam." He didn't turn to look at me. "I am doing my best to do damage control on the situation but if Kyle dies or his parents sue, there's nothing I can do to keep you out of court."

"You think *I* did this?" I screamed at him.

"We're not going to tell your mother. Alright? She has enough to worry about."

"Dad, it's- I- Kimber- it was fucking Prescott! And Sheriff Clery!"

"Yes, you arrived at the hospital in Killian's truck. We already talked to them both."

I was so frustrated and full of rage that my next words came out a jumbled, stuttering mess that ended in a helpless scream. We pulled into our driveway and my dad turned off the car and finally turned to look at me as I struggled to catch my breath.

"Samuel, we will never speak of this again. Do you understand?"

"Are you fucking kidding me, Dad? Kyle might fucking die. I saw Kimber-"

"Enough! If you want this to go away you will keep your mouth shut about it, make no statements to anyone and I'll hire the best lawyer I can afford to clean up your mess, but you're not going to college until next year. I don't know why you beat your best friend almost to death and frankly I don't want to. You-"

"Fuck you!" I screamed at him and threw open the door to the cruiser. I ran then, away from him and the house and my broken life. He didn't come after me. Not that day or any other.

Since everyone in town thought I was a violent thug no one would let me stay with them when I called around. I eventually went to a motel far outside of town and drained the last of my savings from work paying for the room.

I went back to pick up my car from the trailhead, but it was gone and I hoped it was Kimber who had it and not a tow yard. I read the paper every morning for some mention of Kyle's condition. I saw the Daley's birth announcement about 10 days later. They had just had a son that they named William. The whirling, twirling, Shiny Gentlemen lit up the valley with its stench and song of death that same night and Whitney was gone. It was the last time I ever heard it.

I stayed in Drisking long after the money had run out and I was sleeping on the concrete behind the motel. I stayed until Kyle was released from the hospital; a mute, empty-eyed, soulless vegetable. I went to see him once, while only Parker was home, and threatened him until he let me inside the house.

When I had assured myself that the Kyle I knew was dead and only his empty husk remained, I left his house and hitchhiked out of town. And after I spent four drunken, drug-fueled years in Chicago, I came home one day to find a letter waiting for me. It didn't have a return address but it was postmarked California.

I knew it was from her before I'd even picked it up. She'd written so many of my assignments for me that I knew Kimber's handwriting better than my own.

Inside it was a letter. *The* letter. I read it only once, many years ago, until I sat down to transcribe it today.

My Kimber,

I need to tell you some things before I go. I know you aren't going to understand why we did the things we did. Please understand, it was all born out of love, at least it started that way. You're everything to me and you'll always be my daughter. Do you understand? And I'm leaving this world because of what

I've done to you, not because of what you are. I don't want you to be upset about what you are. Because WHO you are is beautiful.

My love, this town has done horrible things. And all of us who live here are guilty. Read this letter and leave this place.

I need to tell you all of this. I need to start at the beginning:

Somewhere along the way, decades ago, the major population of Drisking became unable to bear children. Most people blamed the town for letting the iron ore leak into our water table during the collapsing of our mines.

This is the same water table that still provides the town's water today. They were never quite able to fix it and ore is toxic and exposure causes infertility. The town did, and still does, suffer greatly from its effects.

And the Prescott's, they solved the problem that no one could solve. It was an ugly, crass solution but most people were happy to look away when they were able to raise families again. You see they took girls, mostly women from other places, and they impregnated them and gave us their babies.

And the town came under the care of Thomas Prescott when he started to "sell" some of the babies on the side for a profit to rich couples. And the Sheriff, he helped him do this. But then an ugly rumor started that they were selling to human traffickers. And the Prescott's had to offer triple the price for girls. And in town, we began to murmur. But we once again turned the other cheek when the city was suddenly flooded with money because of how well the traffickers paid. People had well-paying jobs again and were proud to call Drisking home. So we said nothing and those that did were taken to the mountain.

Because that is where they do it. There is a place on the mountain where the women are taken, Kimber: Drifters, runaways and, if their parents choose it, sometimes the girls in town are even sold back. They arrange to sell the girls and they meet them at a tree halfway between our town and their baby mill. Sometimes kids play there now. I think you played there.

The Prescott's and the Sheriff are the ones who impregnate the girls and the children are named after them. P children for the Prescotts and K children for the sheriff. And then when the women become too sick or too old to deliver profitable babies they are sent through a giant machine that was used to refine ore. They call it "the Shiny Gentleman". Their bodies are crushed and the blood and skin stripped away and what remains of them are their stolen children and the dust of their bones. And all that's left of their bodies is the powder that they spread over the mountain to hide our crimes.

I'm telling you this, Kimber, because you are one of those children. Most of your friends are one of those children.

Please get out of Drisking before your father finds this letter. Run away and never come back and never speak of it to anyone. Their industry has deep roots now and the traffickers have lofty connections. Don't tell anyone. Don't keep this letter. Don't look back.

I love you. I'm sorry I have to leave you. We all have to answer for our sins and I'm ready to burn in hell for mine.

Love always and forever,
Mom

ABOUT THE AUTHOR

C.K. Walker lives in Salt Lake City, Utah where she skis, hikes and travels extensively in between her nightmares. For new stories and content please visit: https://www.facebook.com/pages/C-K-Walker/1503387386575559.

Walker

Made in the USA
Middletown, DE
21 September 2024

61225932R00110